LIFE'S MANY JOURNEYS

BOOK TWO

THE NEW LIFE SERIES

BY LOUISE BOUCK

PERMISSION

Scripture quotations taken from The HOLY BIBLE, NEW INTERNATIONAL VERSION® NIV® Copyright © 1973, 1978, 1984, 2011 by Biblica, Inc. ™ Used by permission. All rights reserved.

TABLE OF CONTENTS

ACKNOWLEDGEMENTS

It is important to say thank you to all the people who have encouraged me. A special shout out to Mary Koestner. Thank you for your prayer support and subtle questions that helped me to release the stories God had tucked in my heart.

A big thank you goes to my husband, Dale Bouck who managed to keep my computer running in spite of the monsoons while being a willing editor. Thank you to my family members that suffered through reading very rough drafts. A big thank you hug to R. J. Dick who was the first to want to read the story of Ben Slater in "More Than Survival" and to Brenda Dick who read "The Story of Sarah" to RJ when he was ill, and thanks to Donna Shaw, who enthusiastically helped me to keep Sarah's feet on the right path.

Thank you to Ray Shaw for his help and patience when I was confronted by new technology. Without his expertise and encouragement, my stories would still just be files in my computer.

Thank you to the staff at the computer lab for their help. What would any of us do without the public libraries and the wonderful people that work there?

DEDICATION

This New Life Series is dedicated to Jesus and my family, those that have gone before me, those who are with me and those to come, and all my brothers and sisters in Christ.

†

INTRODUCTION

This is book two in "The New Life Series." The Christian fiction in this series is written to offer the reader a wholesome entertainment, starting back in a simpler but not easier time. The example of spiritual strength and "never quit" attitude is refreshing and inspiring. The pioneer adventurers follow the trail to a new land and challenges they never imagined.

In book one "More Than Survival", follow Benjamin Slater as he copes with the wild isolation of the new frontier and the lessons of self-preservation as he experienced with the pain of loss and joys of accomplishment. He traveled some of "Life's Many Journeys" in book two and learned to appreciate the "Land's Heritage," in book three.

In book four, you will find out "The Story of Sarah" his missing sister.

As you read the books, Ben develops into a man of physical and spiritual strength. His problem solving mind is challenged many times.

When Sarah, his sister returns to him and they are "Together" in, book five. You will find out how her life affected the Indians that took her and how they became "The Blue Stone People," in book six.

A change of scene takes you to the camp of the Sentu and three survivors enter the story, in book seven "Teewahpanyee the Boy, Two Feathers the Man," Willow and Water Bug bring new strength and young blood to an old people. With Willow at his side in book eight Two Feathers becomes leader of "The People of The Lion". They are chosen by the Lion of Judah to be rescuers, and are rewarded in book nine, by being allowed to discover "The Lion's Den."

In book ten, the land that Ben Slater's father chose has miraculously remained with the family as time has evolved and generations were born.

In a day beyond today, book ten skips to the final times after the rapture. A new heroine stands up bravely to the soldiers of the anti-Christ. She finds Ben's Bible, Mary Slater's journals and the gift of faith. Emily spreads the Holy Word and struggles to survive the time of tribulation as she finally realizes that this is "Just the Beginning" for those who believe.

PROLOGUE

When Benjamin Slater's father decided to leave the rest of the wagon train, he had no idea of the events that he had set in motion.

An Indian raiding party observed the single covered wagon leave the train. They watched. It was easy to anticipate their destination.

Three of the Indians rode ahead, staying out of sight.

Josiah had chosen the largest oak tree visible. Sarah, their nine-year-old daughter, Ben's sister, rode inside and he, nearing sixteen, sat on the back with feet hanging down from the covered wagon.

As they stopped the raiders fiercely attacked.

Later working through his pain, Ben buried his parents and searched for his sister. She was gone and so were the horses, his father's rifle and most of the things that had been in the wagon.

The serious challenge of his situation took him to his knees. With the same strong faith that had encouraged his family to move west, Ben called on God for wisdom and strength. In the coming months he built a shelter, learned to hunt without a gun and to gather food.

During the summer he created a new and different family. Ben filled most of that season with short trips of exploration, learning the food sources available.

In late autumn a friend came and became a big brother to Ben. Asked to stay on, they enjoyed Christmas together and planned a garden and a journey for spring.

Now on the journey they followed the Hickory River as it narrowed and ran between high walls and then tumbled to a deep blue pool before moving on over rapids and finally returning to the calm river that seemed more like the river that Ben recognized. They stopped to camp on the edge of the dense virgin forest.

Their current goal was to cross the Silver River and visit Jed's friends.

CHAPTER ONE   THE SILVER

Morning brought a strong wind and dark clouds. The smell of rain was in the air. They ate a quick meal of travel cakes and headed out as soon as they had packed up their camp.

"If we make good time we can get to the Silver River before noon, then it is probably another half day hike to get to a place where we can cross safely," said Jed. "The Silver is tricky and she is always changing. She brings in several channels toward the end and deep mud in between."

"Ginger has had enough of that stuff to last her a lifetime," said Ben.

"Farther up it merges into one and not so deep that we can't cross. It's taking us a little longer than I thought it would. It's faster in the canoe," said Jed.

As the storm passed overhead Ben acknowledged that they had escaped a soaking as he pointed to the sky.

"I hope it didn't dump a lot of water into the Silver farther north."

"She flattens out and goes shallow and sandy for a while," said Jed. "We can keep testing the bottom and find a place to cross." They decided to cut across the forest floor, away from the Hickory, hoping to meet the Silver far enough up river for a safe crossing. When they emerged from the forest at the edge of the Silver River, it appeared as wide as a small lake.

"Well I guess we know that the storm dumped a lot of water north of here," said Jed. "I can't believe it is this big. If we go up farther maybe it will be better."

Ben was afraid of how Ginger would act if he tried to swim her across water that wide. He wouldn't consider endangering her.

They continued to move north until it was late afternoon. The width of the river began to diminish. On the other side they could see gravel banks still under the water. The water came up to the edge of the forest just ahead of them. Jed realized that they had nearly walked to the mud bog. As they reached that point, they could see that the water was clear and the bottom was covered with stones and gravel.

"It's a lot wider than normal here but the current isn't too strong. The middle is too deep to walk though. She will have to swim some of the way. Do you think she will do it?" asked Jed.

"Sure, but I think it would be easier for her without all the stuff on her back. Let's make a raft and after we take her across, we can return and push the raft across."

"Let's wait and do it first thing in the morning. We are all tired now," suggested Jed. "The water will go down some more during the night and that way if our stuff gets a little wet, it will dry out as we walk. We can camp here and then start fresh."

"We might as well make a fun evening of it," said Ben, agreeing with the plan.

"Let's hunt and see what we can get for a fresh meal."

As soon as they started to remove the packs from Ginger's back, Stump took that as his signal of permission to explore.

"I think this is the part of the trip that Stump likes best," chuckled Jed. They quickly set up camp and made a stone ring for a campfire, and collected twigs and branches for the fire. They fed their coal to be sure it would stay alive but didn't want to light a campfire until they were there to watch it. Ben got his bow and joined Jed. They entered the trees in the same direction Stump had disappeared. Suddenly they could hear Stump barking in the distance.

"I think he has scared everything away," said Jed.

"It sounds like he has found something," offered Ben. They hurried through the trees toward the sound.

When they got nearer they could see that he was beside a person on the ground.

"What is someone doing way out here alone?" yelled Ben, as they ran to help.

"It is a woman!" said Jed. "She has been hurt! Ben, carry my gun and I will carry her back to camp." She moaned when Jed lifted her, but she didn't open her eyes.

Stump ran around them in circles, whining. He had known that the woman needed help. Ben praised him.

"Good boy Stump. I wonder how she got here."

"She is so thin. She is like carrying a child," said Jed, as he hurried back to camp with the woman cradled in his arms. It was easy to see that her clothes were dirty and worn.

"She must have been lost in the woods for quite a while," said Ben, as they made their way through the trees.

Jed placed the woman gently on his bedroll.

"She has a high fever. We need to bring the fever down."

"First let's ask God to help," said Ben. Jed and Ben knelt beside her. They had already been praying all the way back to camp. Now Ben prayed out loud.

"Please God, you sent us into the woods to find this poor lady. Please help us now to know what to do for her. Help Jed to find the right medicines for her to make her well. Give her strength and please heal her, Father."

"Thank you Father," added Jed, as he hurried away.

"Amen," said Ben.

Ben sponged her face and arms with the cold river water. He trickled a little into her mouth, but she didn't swallow. It ran across her cheek and onto the bed.

Jed was moving quickly along the riverbank looking for the right plants, and then he headed into the woods, checking plants here and there as he went. Ben was worried.

Jed returned with his arms loaded with different plants. Ben had started the fire and had two pans of water heating.

"Good you have the fire going. I found this plant with the white flowers. It will bring her fever down better than willow bark, but it also can affect her heart so I have to be careful not to use too much. She is so weak. This one helps to build the blood. She needs nourishment. If I could get her awake, then I could get her to drink. She is so hot! I think I know what I am going to do." He pulled off his leather clothes and picked the woman up and carried her into the river. He sat down on the edge with the water splashing at his waist. He held her against his chest and continually cupped water up over her hair and back until she felt cooler.

As he sat there holding her on his lap in the water, he instructed Ben on how to make an infusion of the White flowers, and how to brew the tonic into a tea.

"It will be very bitter. We will need to add mint. I wish we had some of your honey to add. Could you also crush some of the dried meat and make a rich broth, or maybe you should just use the travel cakes. Never mind the meat. I think she is a lot cooler now. Would you bring me the quilt to lay her on?" She seemed to stir a little as he put her on the quilt. Jed propped her up with his arm and Ben handed him the cup with the infusion. Jed tested it against his lip for temperature and strength.

"You did a good job Ben. It is just as I remember it."

Her eyes fluttered and then opened at the sound of his voice.

"Hello," Jed said, turning on his most beautiful smile. "We are going to help you. This is medicine. You need to drink some of it." She swallowed a little before her eyes closed and she slipped back into darkness.

"She wasn't really awake, but I was hoping that I could reach her on some level, enough that she would drink all of this. Guess I better put all my clothes back on in case she does wake fully. A man in soggy underwear would probably frighten her." Jed returned to her side and lifted her head again and again, spooning tiny amounts of medicinal liquid into her mouth.

She became burning hot with fever again as soon as her worn, torn dress began to dry out a little. This time he got a pan of water from the river and wet the quilt wrapping her in it. The cold water caused her to stir and he took the small opportunity to ladle some of the bitter tonic in her mouth followed by a spoon of the broth Ben had made. She moaned now and then, but there was no other sound from her.

Stump wouldn't leave her side. He nudged her and whined.

"He knows her, Ben. They have to be from the same wagon train. Was she on yours? Do you recognize her?"

Ben looked at the small face and dull stringy hair and his eyes were filled with disbelief.

"She could have been, but that doesn't seem possible. The woman I remember looked much younger. They would have killed her and if they didn't, the winter would have. It's been more than a year! How could she survive all winter?"

"I can't answer that. I wonder how old she is. She looks a lot older than either of us," said Jed. As Ben sat on the grass beside the fire he reached over and offered Stump a piece of jerky, but Stump wouldn't take it. He stayed next to the woman all night.

Her temperature peaked in the middle of the night, as she mumbled words they couldn't understand. By morning it had come down a bit. Jed felt her head and it was still hotter than normal, but much better than it had been. He sponged her head and arms again, but now more because it made him feel he was doing something for her. He put his ear to her chest and her heartbeat was strong. He decided to try to get her to take some more of the infusion. He spooned it into the corner of her mouth, first the tonic, next the broth until he felt he had done all he could for the time being.

He asked Ben to wake him if anything changed and he finally lay on the grass beside her and slept.

13

The sun rose above the river causing a bright glare. The campsite was flooded with sunshine. Jed opened his eyes, only moments before she did. She looked around but couldn't figure out where she was. She tried to raise her head but instantly the world began to spin and nausea hit her stomach. Jed urged her to lay back and softly he soothed and reassured her that she was safe and that she was going to be all right.

Ben came with a cup of water and spooned water into her mouth. She swallowed it. He did the same with the broth, and she swallowed again before she closed her eyes. This time it seemed that she was sleeping and not unconscious. He stroked her hair back from her face and felt the fever.

Jed went for a dip in the river just long enough to scrub all over, while Ben made tea and started a pan of soup cooking. He picked greens that he recognized and added them, along with cattail roots. They would not be moving on for at least a few days, until she was stronger.

First he started a pan of mash. He wanted to be sure they had cooked what she could eat when she was able. He discovered a small pouch of sugar He had tucked in at the last minute before they left. He didn't remember putting it there until he saw it. He added some to the bitter medicine.

Ben knew that the lion skin needed processing and was glad to have a project. He scraped until it was totally clean and began to soften. The predator had stalked them on the trail. Ben was glad that Jed was a good shot. Ben pegged it out in the grass under the trees and left it there in the shade.

As he worked, he had been lost in thought about the wagon train and the sad events of that day.

He heard Jed softly speaking to her. She was awake and looking at him. He explained who they were and where they were going. He asked her name but she couldn't answer. She was so weak. He wasn't sure if she comprehended anything he had said. He spooned some broth in her mouth, then tonic. She gagged, but knew that it was medicine and tried to swallow it. Next he gave her a spoon of water. She needed liquid badly. He tried one more spoon of water, but she had fallen asleep.

They picked up the bedding by the corners and slowly carried it with her on it, into the shade under the trees. She didn't wake. Stump had been panting, but now got a drink from the river before returning to her side to maintain his vigil.

Once more Ben offered him a piece of jerky and again he refused it. Ben put a pan of water near him and left the jerky beside it. Now that they were caring for the woman, Ben wondered why Stump continued to guard her. He was watching over her as if he had found someone that he had lost.

He pulled the counting stick from his bundle.

"Today is Sunday!"

"Forgive us Lord for not being more aware of your holy day. We ask that you give us all your rest and your blessings. Specially give your blessing of health to this woman and bless our hands so that we do the right things to aid in her healing."

He opened his Bible and there before him was Matthew 4:23 NIV.

"Jesus went throughout Galilee, teaching in their synagogues, preaching the good news of the kingdom, and healing every disease and sickness among the people."

"Thank You, Lord, for hearing me and giving me an answer that I couldn't miss. You are a good God and true to your word. You are the same today and forever. You are a merciful and healing God. We thank you and praise You, Lord."

He continued to read audibly but softly. For a long time the words of the scripture drifted through the trees of the campsite. He pulled the mash and soup away from the fire and made a pot of coffee. When he looked over at the woman he saw that her eyes were open. Ben hurried to her side with fresh water and spooned it into her mouth. Her lips were cracked and dry from the fever. He came back with a bit of grease and dabbed it on gently.

Jed felt her head and it was cooler.

"How do you feel?" He asked her.

"Tired," was the whispered answer, "and thirsty." He spooned more broth into her mouth, then tonic, followed by water. She accepted whatever he offered. He felt she was improving.

Stump stood up and bent close to her face. She had not been aware of him until then. A feeble smile touched her lips.

"My good boy," she whispered, as she fell asleep again.

"She does know him. What do you make of that?" said Jed. "He had to be with her. She recognized him!"

Ben's heart skipped a beat as he realized that she would want to keep the dog with her, and he could lose Stump.

Jed left camp with his rifle asking Ben to give her water and broth whenever she woke.

Ben took off his clothes and jumped in the water and scrubbed with the sand until he suddenly saw that he was making his skin raw. He was so upset at the thought of losing Stump that it was the only thing he could think of.

"Forgive me God, for being selfish. I know that she has lost her family and everything. I know that she loves him. I could see that. Please help me to deal with this." Ben pushed the water from his skin and pulled his clothes back on. He flipped his dripping hair to the back of his head and ran his fingers through it to remove the tangles, before pulling it back and tying it with the leather strip. He felt refreshed, but definitely not at peace.

Jed came back into camp with a small deer over his shoulders.

"I thought fresh meat might help her to get her strength back," he said. Jed had cleaned the deer, but the skin was still on it.

He walked over into the shade and looked down at the sleeping woman, gently touching her face. It was still too warm, but she was getting better. Stump watched his every move. Jed reached over and put the pan of water between the dog's paws. He took a long drink. As Jed moved the pan back, Stump licked his hand as if to say, thank you.

They made a support for the deer to suspend over the fire, on a large green branch. Ben added pieces of wood to the fire, and then started to work the lion skin again using some of the fat from the young deer. He had taken the hide off and laid it beside the lion's skin.

"Maybe we can make her some sort of a dress thing," he said Jed was already scraping the deer hide.

"Do you think if we made something like a short sleeved shirt, only longer, that it would work for her?" Jed asked.

"I don't know why not. We could braid a thin belt for her and she could tie it around her waist to make it fit better," said Ben. "We can have it done before she is strong enough to travel. Her shoes are worn through on the bottom. They are over there."

"We can make new soles on them," suggested Jed.

The next day, she had been able to sit up, talk a bit and eat soup and even a tiny amount of deer meat. Jed and Ben didn't question her. They thought that she would tell her story when she was strong enough.

It was her third day in camp before she was ready to say that her name was Elizabeth Ann Wilson.

"My husband was killed with the others on the wagon train. Scruff was our dog. I thought that he had been killed, too. I saw an arrow hit him. The Indians took many things from the wagons and then burned them. I ran, but one grabbed me and took me on his horse. He was an ugly big beast, with all that paint on his face. He wasn't cruel to me. Just firm about the way he treated me. I know he intended to take me back to his village to be his wife."

She continued.

"He tied my hands and ankles and pushed me down on his blanket. He had his arm around my waist. I shudder to think about it. He could have been much worse. I waited until he fell asleep and then I stole his knife from his waist and cut the thongs that bound me. I held that knife next to his throat. I wanted to kill him, but something held me back. I inched my way into the trees and ran all night, going back to the burned wagons. I stayed hidden during the day, in the tall grass nearby, or under one of the wagons that still stood. It wasn't as burned as the rest.

I buried my husband in a hole that I dug with a cooking spoon. Then I just waited for several days, hoping that someone else would come back to the wagons, too.

I had no survival skills at all when we joined the train but the other women were kind and taught me a few things. I learned to make a fire and how to cook a rabbit over a campfire. I was learning which greens were edible when the Indians struck the train."

Ben patted her hand, not really knowing how to comfort her.

"We know you are tired. You don't have to talk anymore now."

"No, I want to. I need to tell you."

"When I finally came to the conclusion that I would be safer if I moved into the woods, I gathered up what few things I could find and carry. I still had his knife. I found a bowl, a water bag and one thin blanket that I had to remove from the shoulders of an old lady that had been walking beside her wagon."

"So you were in the woods all winter?" asked Jed. "How did you survive the cold? What did you eat?"

"There was a grass fire, and I was on the plains when that storm went through. I got some meat there, and dried a lot, all I could carry. I slept in the open along the wagon trail. It didn't make much sense I guess to follow the path our wagon would have taken, but it gave me a direction. I didn't want to go back. When I came to the river I could see the trail on the other side so I swam across, but then I started to follow the river looking for a place that I could just crawl into. This side turns into mud flats as far as I could see. For two days of walking it was like that. The bank on the other side of the river is higher. I climbed a tree and I was able to see a bluff peeking out of the trees on this side, way back in the woods, and I decided that it was a chance worth taking so I had to swim back over. The woods were deeper than I thought and it took another day and a half to get to the bluff."

Elizabeth continued.

"There is a small cave about half way up, not much bigger than a wagon inside, but large enough for me. It has a narrow slit of an opening, and that was good because it helped keep the wind out. Getting wood up there was really hard work, but at least I had sense enough to stockpile lots in there."

"All that time, what did you eat?" asked Ben, eager to find out what she had done in circumstances worse than his had been.

"I ate grass and some plants and roots the women had shown me," she said. "The meat from the prairie fire spoiled, because I was getting it wet and carrying it around in the blanket. The first rabbit, I actually caught was very small. I kept it for a couple days, and then I let it go."

"After that I learned to throw stones hard enough to down rabbits and squirrels, too. That worked in the summer, but it is harder to see anything to eat in the winter. I found a tree with nuts on it and I carried my skirt full of them up to the cave, until I had a big pile. I think they are what kept me alive. I learned to fish with a line made from threads I pulled from the blanket and a pin from my hair. I caught some but my cave and fire were too far from the river to make that a practical solution until I learned to dry them. I would stay at the river for several days and then take them back, but when I got back squirrels had stolen a lot of my nut pile."

She continued, "When I got back to my cave late last fall I was sitting at the fire pit trying to start a fire and a black bear came in the cave. She went to the back, curled up and went to sleep. She didn't even look at me. She was half asleep when she came in. I crept out and had to find another place. It was really hard. The winter nearly killed me. The second cave wasn't as big and the doorway was wider. I piled rocks in the opening to block some of the wind. At least it was up high enough so that the snow was below the opening. It was harder to keep warm. My nuts were in with the bear, so I had to start over. It was difficult to find many. The ones left in the trees were challenging to reach. I found some wild apples on a few branches of one tree. Anyway I'm alive, thanks to you, and here now, and that's about all I can remember."

"Beth, that's a fantastic story," said Jed. "Now I think you should rest. You don't want to tire yourself. You still aren't well." He had automatically shortened her name without thinking about it.

"That's what James called me," she said, and started to cry. Jed wrapped his arms around her and leaned her against his chest and rocked until she was finally quiet.

When he looked down at her, he realized that she had fallen asleep in the security of his arms wrapped around her. He grasped that he had given her the only comforting that she had felt since that terrible day.

CHAPTER TWO   FEELING BETTER

Jed gently tipped her back onto the bed and wiped his eyes with the back of his hand. He was embarrassed to find tears there. He had felt her fear as she told her story and felt her pain at the loss of her loved one. He sat studying her face and discovered that he cared about her very much. He was so glad that they had found her.

When he thought of all she had been through, it made a painful knot form in his chest. She has a strong will to live, a fighter is what she is, he thought.

Stump was eating again, now that he saw that she was getting better. Stump studied the woods for a moment then trotted off in the direction he had been looking.

"I think he has finally decided to end his self-imposed vigil," said Jed.

"That is the best sign we have had yet, that she is getting better!"

"Yes he sure is sensitive to her condition. He is a good dog," mumbled Ben, "I will miss him terribly."

"Well he isn't going anywhere yet, so cheer up, little brother. You know God always has a good plan." Their meal from the deer was juicy and delicious. They ate heartily. While she had been so ill they had skipped eating several times. Now, like Stump, they had given themselves permission to return to a more normal routine.

In the morning, Beth sat up for a while and even asked for a pan of water so she could wash up a little. They warmed some and gave her a piece of soft leather to use. Then they served her soup and hot deer meat. Jed insisted she take more of the bitter tonic. She didn't want it because of the nasty taste, but knew that he was doing his best to make her well. He gave her a small cup of coffee to sip and she enjoyed it.

"I always liked coffee and I missed it. It's strange, some of the things I longed for in that cave. Coffee was one of them and ice cream, even though it was freezing cold. I kept thinking about strawberry ice cream."

She got up with Ben's help and walked slowly around the campsite, leaning heavily on his arm.

"You are doing so well. We are glad that you are feeling better. When you get your strength back we will take you to meet Tom and Gentle Fawn. You can probably stay there until you can find a way back home," said Jed.

"I am sorry. I have been such a burden," she said softly. "I have held you up on your journey. You have done so much for me. You and Ben saved my life. As soon as I am strong enough you can just tell me the way to the settlement. I am sure I can make it on my own. I don't want to hold you up any longer than I have. If I have learned one thing from all this, it is that I need to able to be on my own!"

"Wait," said Jed. "I didn't mean that I wanted to get rid of you! You're wrong! You aren't a burden! We like having you around, and that happens to be where we are going. It's not out of our way, so relax. It's just that they are the nicest people in the whole world and I know they will want you to stay. Besides, they live at a point where the rivers join so you have twice the chance of meeting up with people that are heading back east."

"I'm sorry Jed. I guess I am defensive. You see; I don't want to go back east. I really want to find a way to stay out here. All I have ever wanted is a simple place where I could live my life without people judging me. I want to grow my own garden and raise a bunch of wonderful, noisy children. My father owns a large mercantile back east and my mother is so busy having parties and having more of everything than everyone else that she hasn't time to really see what life is all about. God didn't mean us to live like that. They could do so much good for others if they would only open their eyes and see all the need. They said that if I married James and left with him, they never wanted to hear from me again. James wanted the same things that I did. Our wagon wasn't full of fancy furniture. It was full of things for a farm. We bought a plow just before we left. We even had a cage of chickens!" She started to cry again and this time Jed knew that she needed to be allowed to release her anger and grief. She had held it in far too long.

"It is natural to cry," he said softly. "You have been through so much. You need time to start healing more than your body. Your spirit has been wounded, too." He went for a walk along the river and gave her time alone for her tears. He was scanning the edge of the woods, always aware of his environment, when he spotted something red down in the grass. He knelt down and collected a small handful of ripe wild strawberries. In a couple days there would be lots of ripe ones but right now it was all he could find.

He returned to camp with his treasure. "I have a present for you," he said. "Hold out your hand." As she did, he dropped the little berries into her palm.

"These are strawberries! They are my favorite things, in the entire world!" Jed laughed at her enthusiasm. She was easy to please.

As she nibbled the berries, she watched as Ginger munched the grass nearby.

"She is a beautiful horse. We had good horses. They were big and strong, good for farm work. They were not beautiful but James said he didn't need them to look great if they were healthy, good natured, strong and willing to pull a wagon or a plow."

"Ginger is a good horse," said Jed. "She is gentle and smart. She hasn't been ridden yet. She is about a year old I guess. He got her by pulling her out of the mud bog. She would have died if he hadn't come along when he did. She is from wild mustang stock, but you would never know it by her sweet and friendly disposition."

"You two seem to make a habit of coming along when you are needed!"

"Beth, where did Ben go? I haven't seen him all afternoon."

"I haven't either." Just then Stump came bounding up and Ben followed a few feet behind him. Stump gave Beth a wet kiss and almost knocked her over. He acted as if he had found her all over again with extreme wiggles, whimpers and wags.

"He sure likes you," said Ben.

"Where have you been all afternoon? I was getting a little worried," asked Jed.

"Stump and I have been exploring. There is a clearing in the woods and it is covered with wild flowers. Here Beth, I picked these for you," he said, as he brought them from behind his back with a flourish.

"Oh, they are beautiful! Look how many different kinds and colors! Thank you, Ben. That was so thoughtful of you. They smell so sweet. Thank you," she said again as she gave him a quick hug.

"Jed, I had an idea. Do you think Ginger would let Beth ride on her if we took some of the other stuff off? We could carry some of the load. Beth is so little that I don't think it would overload Ginger," said Ben.

"She would need to let Ginger get to know her first.

I'm not sure how we should go about it," said Jed, with a big smile, "but let's try." Ben went over and got Ginger. He brought her to Beth and Jed got a pan with some grain.

"Ginger, we want you to meet Beth," said Ben, formally. Beth was delighted with the sweet way that Ginger blew at her hand and nuzzled it, taking the opportunity to get her scent.

"She is looking for a treat. Here, give her this," said Ben. Ben held the pan up so that Ginger could eat the grain and still get her ears scratched by Beth at the same time.

"I think they will be good friends. Ginger seems to like her," said Jed. Ben immediately started to work with Ginger. Resting on her shoulders, he would lean heavily on her back while he brushed her, getting her used to the idea of humans on her back. He hugged her neck and slid onto her back and just sat there leaning forward scratching. She didn't mind at all.

24

The next morning, Beth said, that she was strong enough to sit on Ginger. Jed gently lifted her up on top of the quilt. She sat there and hugged Ginger's neck patting and scratching, copying what Ben had done.

"Ginger let's go." Ben urged her forward slowly. She followed him all around the campsite.

"I think she is willing to carry you, but it will be at the same walk she uses to carry the packs, and all her direction will come from us and the lead rope."

"That's fine. I feel privileged that she will accept me so easily. You are such a good girl. Such a good, Ginger," she said, giving her more scratches.

After the activity with Ginger, they ate and Beth lay down. Ben and Jed had worked on the skins every day while Beth napped. They were soft and ready to be used. Ben used his shirt as a pattern. He cut her dress smaller and a little longer, cutting fringe on the bottom. The sleeves were an extension of the shoulder and fringed along the edge. Jed worked on the stitching while Ben cut new soles for her shoes from the edge of the tent hides. They sipped coffee and sewed. When the clothes were finished they were rolled up and put inside one of the packs. Ben and Jed were saving them for a little surprise.

It hadn't rained for over a week. The river had returned to its normal appearance of a rippling silver ribbon that had inspired its name. In the morning, they set to work building a raft. They packed up the camp, remembering to put a coal in the firebox.

"Let's take the packs and stuff across first so we can test how the current pulls on the raft before we try to take Beth across," suggested Jed. They put everything in the middle of the raft on top of the tent. They pulled their leather clothes off behind some bushes and put on old cloth pants they had brought along for that purpose. Ben had grown a lot during the winter and found his trousers were very tight at the waist. They hurried into the cold water. The current was swift and pulled hard on the raft. Soon the raft and the men were bobbing in the middle, heading down stream. It was impossible to control it. The river swung wide, sending the raft toward the opposite shore and at that point they were able to catch a footing, regaining control. They walked in the shallow water, guiding the raft back to an area where the riverbank rose gradually. Once their bundles were unloaded they fastened the rope to the raft. They swam back bringing the rope.

From the shore they were able to pull the empty raft back quite easily. Ginger stood nearby stomping her feet. She had figured out that she was going to be asked to cross the river and was nervous about it.

"We better take her next. She is getting frightened. I don't want to have to catch her if she bolts," said Ben.

"How do you want to do it?" asked Jed. "The same as we did before when we crossed the Hickory with one on each side of her?"

"Sure," said Ben. "That worked last time, only this time she will have to swim the middle part."

"I better be on the down-stream side. I think I'm a little stronger swimmer," said Jed.

"I beat you last time we raced or have you forgotten?" teased Ben.

"Well, I was trying," laughed Jed. "Let's do it." He tied a short piece of rope around her neck with an end trailing on either side, for something additional to grasp, if needed.

"Come on, Ginger, let's go," Ben said firmly, and started into the water with one arm around her neck and his other hand holding the rope. He thought that his closeness would give her security.

Jed walked on her other side with his hand gripping the rope on her neck, leaving his left hand free to stroke and swim. She was fine until she couldn't touch bottom. She struggled to swim. Trying to stay above the water, she was kicking awkwardly and caught Ben in the upper thigh with her front hoof. The pain sent him reeling. He went under.

With the thrashing horse between them, Jed was unaware of what had happened.

Beth saw it and yelled but Jed couldn't hear her. She ran in and dove under, pushing Ben to the surface. She struggled against the current until he could get a breath and began to swim again. Ben and Beth ended up on the far bank exhausted. Ben was coughing and Beth lay very still. The current had pulled Jed and Ginger down around the bend before they were able to get their footing. Jed led Ginger down the shallow edge to the point they had pulled out the raft to find his two companions collapsed on the bank.

"What happened? Beth, why didn't you wait for the raft? Ben, are you all right?" Ben continued to cough but nodded, yes. Beth sat up and tried to explain but she was shivering so badly that her teeth were chattering. Jed wrapped her in the quilt and tossed Ben his dry clothes. As they pulled off their soggy trousers, behind a bush, Jed noticed the huge, round, purple mark developing on Ben's leg. "Wow! She really clipped you a good one, didn't she?" Jed quickly pulled his clothes on over his wet body, and got on his traveling shoes.

"I'll be right back," he said. "He ran back along the river toward the bend. He had seen some plants with purple flowers. They were just what he needed to numb the pain in Ben's leg. He picked several, crushing them between two stones. He placed them on the still growing, huge, purple lump.

"Well at least the flowers match the bruise," joked Ben. Jed fastened the poultice on with a scrap of the deer hide, wrapping it around Ben's leg.

"Pull your pants on carefully and after a few minutes that should feel a lot better."

Jed walked over to the packs and took out the new dress and newly soled shoes that he and Ben had worked on. He handed them to Beth.

"These are for you. We worked on them while you were taking your naps and getting well. We hope that they will fit well enough so that you can use them. They are just a little surprise from both of us." She was delighted and appreciated the practical and much needed gift.

"Thank you so much. You are both amazing," she said as she hugged each of them. Ben noticed that Jed's hug took a little longer, and he smiled to see a small sign of what he already suspected. Jed and Beth were falling in love, and they didn't even know it yet.

Beth tiptoed behind the bushes, wrapped in the trailing quilt and carrying her new clothes.

When she stepped into view she was wearing the dress and the biggest smile she had ever shown them.

"It's perfect. I love it, and my shoes feel so much better. Thank you again for everything." Her eyes were shining with tears, ready to spill. As one escaped to her cheek, Jed reached over with his thumb and gently wiped it away.

"I hope those are happy tears," he said grinning.

"Yes Jed, I am very happy."

CHAPTER THREE   THE TWINS

Ben discovered that the poultice was numbing the pain in his leg. He was eager to get moving before it started to hurt badly again. He fed Ginger some grain and gave her scratches, and then he helped Jed create two backpacks from Ginger's side packs. The quilt was folded over the lion's skin and then it was spread on Ginger's back. The tent with their bedding formed a roll that was secured on Ginger's back after Beth was lifted up.

Stump had paddled across with no trouble. He had jumped in the same time Beth did. He didn't know quite what was going on but he was sure he didn't want to be left out of it or left behind. Jed gave jerky to everyone, and they slowly started out. He gathered bunches of the purple flowers and tucked them in the bedroll behind Beth. He knew they would be needed before nightfall. Jed washed in the river several times and rubbed his hands on the sand of the bank and on the grass. His fingers were numb from picking the flowers.

Beth was curious about the firebox. She had seen Jed feed it a couple of times, as they moved along.

"That is the cleverest thing I have ever seen!" she said. "I certainly could have used that last winter." Jed smiled broadly and was pleased with her praise and enthusiasm.

By late afternoon, Ben was limping badly. When a dense group of trees and rocks offered some protection from the strong breeze, they decided to stop.

"Ben, sit down and take it easy and I will set up camp," offered Jed. Gratefully, Ben sat on a rock and rested his leg. He could tell that it was badly swollen because his leather pant leg was tight. Jed started a fire and spread out the bedding. The tent wasn't needed over them, but the wind was uncomfortable so he put it up as a wind break to the side. They could immediately feel a relief.

He sliced off pieces of the travel cakes and put the water bags where they could reach them. Stump had gone off exploring as soon as they had stopped. He returned with a rabbit. Jed skinned it and handed it back to him, with lavish praise and scratches. He scraped the skin enough to remove the tissue and rolled it up. They could process it when they arrived at Tom and Gentle Fawn's. He wasn't sure, but he thought they should get there by the next afternoon. They had been moving very slowly.

Jed made mint tea and after pouring two wooden cups full, he added willow bark and chamomile that he had in his pack. He knew that Ben was in pain. He crushed another plant and helped him modestly change into his cloth pants. Jed had cut the legs off so that they didn't bind on Ben's wound and it made it easier for him to put them on. He changed the poultice. Ben's leg was swollen and a very dark purple mark in the shape of Ginger's hoof was raised on the front of his thigh. Ben drank every drop of the tea, hoping for enough relief so that he could fall asleep. The plant began to numb the area and he did drift off.

Beth was wide-awake, staring at the stars. She reached over and took Jed's hand.

"You have been so wonderful to me. How can I ever repay you?" she said softly. "It is so nice to have you with me and not be alone and afraid." She slid closer, until her head rested against his arm. There she fell asleep.

Jed felt a tug at his heart. He did not want to leave her behind when he left Tom and Gentle Fawn's. He wanted her beside him always. He told himself that he was being a fool. She has been through so much. She was simply being grateful, he thought. I mustn't misread it. She is probably apprehensive about staying there with strangers. When she meets them she will be happy to stay. There is a store there by now. Maybe she can work at the store, until what? She said she doesn't want to go back east. She can't just work at a store forever. She can't build a house. She can't plow land. What could she do alone? I don't want to leave her. Maybe she can come with us. She can at least spend the rest of the summer with us to get strong again. If she doesn't like it there I could take her down to Tom's in the fall in the canoe.

"Lord, please help me know what I am to do," he prayed silently. "I want to follow your plan in this, but Lord, I really don't want to leave her behind. I know I should yield this to you. Lord, you took care of her until I came along. I give her and this situation back to you, but would it be all right if I talk to Ben about it, the first chance I get?" With that thought, Jed finally drifted off to sleep.

The windscreen also blocked the rising sun and it was later than usual when they all woke up. Jed looked over at Beth and she smiled back. She is so beautiful, he thought. How could I have ever thought she looked old? I wonder how old she is.

Ben started to get up and moaned and put his head back down.

"I am going to need a little help this morning, big brother," He said. Jed looked over at Ben's leg and it was swollen even more than the night before and black filled the center of the terrible bruise. He can't possibly walk with that, he thought. He replaced the poultice and made him some more tea with willow bark, including the soft bark in the poultice. He told Ben that he was going to go scout around, while that poultice has time to work but really he wanted to get away from camp so that he could think clearly.

"Father God," he prayed, "I need your help and wisdom. I don't know what I should do. Ben shouldn't walk. Should we stay here until he can walk? We are so close. I know I am not anxious to get there because Beth may not decide to come with me and I don't want to face that. Help me, Father, to do the right thing."

He sat quietly under a pine tree for a long time. When he headed back to camp he still wasn't sure what he should do.

It seemed that, automatically, he moved about the camp, making Ben as comfortable as possible. He rolled the quilt and put it under Ben's knee. Then he went to the fire and put on a kettle of soup. Without realizing it, he had decided to stay, at least for a day. Beth nodded approval without saying anything when she saw him starting to prepare the soup. She left the campsite and returned quickly with some wild onions. She cut those up and added them.

Then she took a wooden bowl from Jed's pack and left the camp again. She returned with it full of wild strawberries.

"They grow on this side of the river, too," she said. She placed the bowl down near Jed. He smiled and ate one.

"Let's save them for desert," he said.

They sat near the fire in the quiet of the morning.

"I am sure I can walk tomorrow, if we go slowly," she offered.

"That's great that you are feeling strong enough," Jed smiled at her. "We will see how he is in the morning." Beth walked over to Ginger and hugged her and scratched her ears as she told her how wonderful it was to ride on her back. She was very fond of her. Stump nudged against her, wanting her attention. She laughed at him and sat down on the ground, giving him a hug. She scratched his tummy and talked to him. She looked down at her leather dress and repaired shoes, and felt like she was in a dream.

"My life was saved, and I have you again, just because they decided to take a journey. How can everything change so much in just a few days?" she mused.

She checked on Ben and he was sleeping. Jed had gone into the woods. She thought she should rest while she could. She put a pot of tea on the edge of the fire to heat and prepared a batch of fresh willow bark from the nearby trees, ready to add, before she crawled onto her bed. Jed returned soon after, to find both his companions asleep.

He prepared the poultice and had it ready, when Ben began to stir. Beth sat up and he handed her a cup of the tea and poured one in his own cup, then added the willow bark and set it close to the flames, so it would boil soon. Ben's leg seemed a little better. Just staying off of it with it elevated and resting was helping.

Suddenly, Stump ran through camp and beyond. Hot on his tail was a black bear. She stopped in the middle of her stride, when she realized that she had run into an area with humans. She hesitated and then turned around and quickly ran back the way she had come.

A few minutes later, Stump returned to camp panting hard. His tongue was hanging out the side of his mouth.

"What were you doing that got that bear so annoyed with you Stump? What's the big idea bringing her back to camp? Did you come for help? I'm sure glad she didn't catch you," said Ben, rubbing the big dog under his chin as he talked to him. Stump went to the edge of the river and took a long drink then flopped down in the shade near Ben.

"You have had your adventure for today, haven't you boy?" said Jed, sympathetically. He served up the soup and gave Stump a large portion, once it had cooled.

The next morning, the little party headed out, with Ginger carrying Ben and half his pack. Beth seemed almost giddy to be walking. Getting on Ginger caused Ben pain, but once up he said he was quite comfortable. They stopped at noon for rest, a piece of travel cake and some water. When they saw the Silver River spreading into four fingers as it reached for the Hickory, they knew they were getting close.

By midafternoon, Jed was surprised to see four buildings ahead. One was the house he had helped build and one was the store that was anticipated. He had no idea that two other families had come along and built houses in the time he had been gone. Ben was impressed.

"It looks like a city!" he declared.

Beth didn't feel eager to reach their destination. She looked from Jed to Ben and felt they were slipping away from her with every step she took.

When they arrived, Jed encouraged Ginger to drink at the river's edge and then tied her on a long rope to a tree. There in the shade she had lots of green grass to munch. He brought her the big pan full of water even before he helped Ben off of her back. Ben hobbled toward the door with Beth at his side.

When Jed let out a shrill whistle, the door burst open. Out poured Tom, Gentle Fawn, and two other adults, as a small boy peeked from behind the woman's skirt. She held a plump baby in her arms.

"Oh Jed, it is so good to see you! Welcome back," said Tom, the biggest man in the group, catching Jed in a bear hug.

"Welcome back Jed," said Gentle Fawn in a sweet alto voice. She hugged him, but in a more reserved manner.

Jed looked at his friends and couldn't contain the joy that it brought him.

"This is my little brother, Ben, and this beautiful lady, is Beth."

"Howdy. It's nice to have you here. These are our friends that built the Trading Post, Jed. You met Sam and Helen just before you left. This tyke is Henry and the baby is Abe."

"Hellos" and "Nice to meet you," were said all around, and then Jed had to tease Gentle Fawn. "Looks like you were waiting for Uncle Jed to come back to have that baby! When is it due?"

"Well, we thought it would be later this summer, but I have grown so big that, perhaps it will be sooner," said Gentle Fawn. And they all laughed.

Her discomfort was apparent as she placed her hand in the middle of her back and waddled into the house easing down in the nearest chair. After her tiring walk, Beth also took the liberty to seek a chair. Ben leaned on one leg for a moment then sat down, too. Helen put her sleeping baby in a cradle, tucked in the corner. She prepared a fresh pot of coffee while they talked about the two other houses that had been built and Tom filled them in on the people's names and stories.

Sam and Helen had planned a house on the back of their store, but it hadn't been built yet. All the men would be working on it as soon as more lumber was brought from Tom's mill. Beth watched the women as they talked animatedly. It was apparent that they were happy although they had no luxuries. I wish my mother could see them, she thought. How different she is.

The baby started to fuss. Helen picked him up and took him into the only bedroom to change and feed him. Jed slipped out and set up their camp. A few minutes later Tom followed him out.

"I apologize that we haven't much room, but we could probably make a bed up in the front room for Beth. Gentle Fawn won't mind."

"No, that's fine. We have been sleeping in a camp for close to two weeks now and it is cozy. She seems to like the security of us close by her."

Jed hurriedly told Tom her story. He didn't want her to overhear him and think he was gossiping.

"I feel protective of her. I don't like to let her out of my sight."

"That is an almost unbelievable story," said Tom.

"Are you sure that protective is all you are feeling toward her? I noticed the way you look at her?"

"I'm concerned," said Jed. "She almost died. Look how terribly thin she is. Ginger accidentally kicked Ben when we swam with her across the Silver. He had to ride and Beth walked from our camp this morning. She is exhausted. This trip hasn't been the lark that Ben and I were thinking it would be."

Jed continued, "We will have been gone longer than we intended. We planted a garden before we left. I hope there is something left when we get back."

"It's not all that bad, Jed, it sounds to me like you are hungry and just as tired as your companions. Let's go in and see what the girls are fixing for supper." Tom swung his big hand up and rested it on Jed's shoulder, giving support and showing affection.

As they entered, Jed knew with a glance that Ben's leg was hurting badly. He needed a new poultice and some willow bark tea right away. Jed took a pan in and put it on the stove and asked Gentle Fawn if he could make some willow bark tea for Ben.

"I'm sorry, that I didn't notice his discomfort. I have herbs that will work to ease the pain, along with the willow bark." She crumbled a few leaves into the heating water.

"Does he have an open wound?" she asked.

"No just a very big, deep bruise the size of a horse's hoof."

"Put some of this on and then the poultice," she said, handing Jed a tin of medicated grease.

"You must tell me what herbs you used, so I can learn," said Jed. She explained in detail. After a few minutes, the tea and medication began to ease Ben's pain.

He sat at the table and enjoyed hearing Tom's prayer of thanksgiving and blessings. "Homemade dumplings and chicken stew, this is delicious! I haven't had chicken in ages," said Ben.

"We have two roosters and twelve hens now," said Gentle Fawn. "We thought on such a happy occasion; as your visit and finding Beth that we would celebrate with a rare treat. I'm glad you are enjoying it."

"Wait until you see the dried apple pie she has cooling!" said Tom, proudly. "It would win a blue ribbon, if we had a fair." They all laughed.

"The food is wonderful. Thank you, Gentle Fawn."

They ended the meal with the promised pie and coffee. As soon as the meal was cleared away, the three young travelers excused themselves and went out to their camp. Faithfully, Jed had fed his coal, and he soon had a small fire going. Beth yawned and said she had to go to bed. Her eyes were closing whether she wanted them to or not. She was asleep as soon as she pulled a fur up over her.

Ben slid in on his back, under the canopy Jed had erected. He was clever at constructing various structures out of the one small tent.

"Thanks," Ben whispered softly as he pulled the rolled up quilt under his sore leg.

Jed sat on the grass near the fire, talking to Stump.

"I don't know if you have caught a meal tonight, my furry friend, so would you like a big piece of the jerky?" Stump took it and wagged his tail. He stayed at Jed's side while he ate it, sensing that his company was a comfort.

Finally Jed had to give in to rest and he sought sleep as a relief from his emotional turmoil. He was sure of only one thing; that he didn't want to leave without Beth.

Just as the dawn was breaking, a small tickle on his cheek woke Jed. During her sleep, Beth had rolled toward him and her head now rested on his shoulder. A strand of her hair was fluffed up against his face. He held perfectly still, not wanting to wake her. Stump had no desire to have them continue sleeping. Fun things were more apt to happen if they were up. He snuggled himself in between Ben and Beth, licking first one and then the other. She woke with a giggle as he tried to push his cold nose into her neck. When she realized she was using Jed's shoulder for a pillow, she sat up and started apologizing. Jed laughed.

"It was truly my pleasure," he said.

He rolled out of his furs and into the brisk morning air. Ginger blew a greeting and he took her a pan of grain and gave her a good brushing. She was still under the tree on a long rope. He took her to the river for a fresh drink and filled the pan with cold water, moving her to a different area with plenty of fresh grass. Ben hobbled over and hugged Ginger's neck and scratched her ears. He thanked Jed for taking good care of her. He was feeling rested, but he still had a big purple lump on his leg that ached with each step and each heartbeat.

"When you want to leave, I will be ready," he said bravely.

"Ben, I want to take Beth with us, for at least the rest of the summer. Would you mind?"

"I have been dreading leaving her," exclaimed Ben. "It is so nice to have her around. But you know, Jed, that we haven't got a real house. Do you think she will mind the way we live?"

"She is not like that, Ben. I think she will like the hut. I hope she will agree to come."

"When should we ask her?"

"Let's ask her right away so she has time to think about it," suggested Ben. Jed didn't want her to think about it. He wanted her to say yes and not have to think about it. When he looked up she was standing a few feet away with a puzzled look on her face.

"What do you want me to think about?"

"About coming with us to our place for the summer," said Jed. "By the fall, Sam and Helen will have their house finished and Tom and Gentle Fawn will have more room, if you want to come back."

"Please say yes, Beth," Ben blurted.

Beth didn't have a chance to answer. Tom came running up to them.

"Beth will you come in and help. Gentle Fawn has been in labor for several hours and the baby is coming soon. Helen needs your help." Beth paled at the thought. She had never seen a baby delivered, let alone help deliver one! She needn't have given a moment of worry. Helen had taken charge and all was ready.

Beth placed a baby blanket near the cook stove to warm it, and made sure they had enough hot water. She went to the basin and scrubbed her hands with soap and water and then asked what else she could do. She held Gentle Fawn's hand and felt her squeeze it very hard as she closed her eyes and prayed.

The next thing she knew, with only a low moan from Gentle Fawn, a baby was in Helen's hands and screaming loudly. Helen laughed with joy.

"Gentle Fawn, you have a son! And God isn't done yet!" She quickly wrapped him in a piece of white cotton cloth and handed him to Beth. She looked up from the beautiful baby boy just in time to see Helen delivering another child, a baby girl!

"You have twins, one of each, and they both look healthy and fat. They are big for twins," said Helen.

"I guess you better warm another blanket." The babies were cleaned and gently rubbed with sweet smelling oil and after diapering them; they were wrapped in the warm, cozy blankets. Their mother was made comfortable, before Tom was allowed in the room. They had taken good care of her too, washing her with warm water and combing her long black hair and leaving it loosely cascading over her shoulders. Gentle Fawn's deep brown eyes sparkled with tears of emotion as she looked from one baby to the other and then up at the two women standing beside her.

"Thank you so much for helping me. You are both forever my sisters now."

Helen added a cute touch by tying a pink ribbon on the corner of one blanket and a blue one on the other. She had been prepared, and was delighted that she got to use both.

The women refused to tell Tom if he had a boy or girl. They said that was Gentle Fawn's privilege, as they stepped out and let him enter.

He couldn't believe his eyes when he saw a baby in each of her arms. "You have a son," she said, "and I have a daughter." Tom kissed her gently and looked at each sweet baby's face with amazement.

"Please," she said, "ask Reverend Brown to come and bless our children and record their names in his book."

"What names would you like?" he asked.

"Did you hear the first baby cry loudly?" she asked.

"Yes, as loud as thunder!"

"That was your son. Let's call him Stormy. His sister should be Anne. I wish to give honor to your mother. Do those names please you?"

"Yes, very much," said Tom.

Tom hurried out the door shouting to everyone that he had a boy and a girl. They laughed because by then, everyone knew. Jed was happy for Tom and Gentle Fawn but he was also happy for himself. Maybe by fall, Reverend James Brown would be able to perform a service for him; he thought smiling, maybe a wedding.

CHAPTER FOUR   THE WEDDING

Jed and Ben wanted to give the new parents a gift. They checked in the trading post, but nothing they could trade for, seemed right. Then Ben laughed out loud.

"Jed, the answer is so obvious. Let's make another cradle. Tom made one. It won't be big enough for two babies for very long."

"Great idea," agreed Jed.

They borrowed tools from Tom and headed into the woods. After cutting, piecing and pegging, they returned with a rough cradle. Then their real expertise was used. Ben worked the bottom board and Jed the headboard. They carved and sanded and carved some more. By nightfall they had finished all but a coat of oil to be rubbed into the smooth wood. Ben had carved forest animals and trees. Jed had carved the river, trees, moon and stars. The cradle was beautiful.

While they were so busy with the bed, Beth had traded the lion skin that Jed had given her. He told her she could trade it for anything she wanted, and so she traded it for a yellow wool blanket. She cut out two generous sized crib blankets. Then she borrowed a needle and pulled threads from the edges to hem them. She sat under the tree with Ginger all day, stitching. While Jed and Ben worked on the cradle, she worked on the blankets. When she finished the two blankets she had a wide strip of blanket left. By cutting it in half and seaming it down the middle, she was able to make a third blanket. This she planned to give to Helen for baby Abe. Beth was exhausted by the time she finished.

Gentle Fawn had spent the day getting used to caring for and nursing two babies. Their household was filled with sleeping and waking babies. Helen helped her to care for them so that she could rest a little in between feedings. Midafternoon, Beth had gone in long enough to help Helen put on a huge pot of stew, made with deer meat, dried vegetables and seasoned with fresh herbs. It bubbled and smelled wonderful.

Jed and Ben carried the cradle through the door of the house and into the bedroom. They held it up so that Gentle Fawn could see the beautiful carvings. She was so touched by their hard work and its beauty that she started to cry.

Tom handed her a handkerchief, laughing.

"Don't cry wife or you won't be able to see the gift that Beth has for you."

Beth held one of the blankets up and laid the other in the new cradle.

"I made you two, one for each twin. This one is for Helen," she said, turning and handing the third blanket to the surprised mother.

"Thank you so much. It will be nice and warm for Abe this winter."

"Thank you for the cradle and the blankets, you are all so kind," said Gentle Fawn.

A man named Joseph, foreman of Tom's lumber crew, tapped on the door frame and stepped in saying, "Tom, I have good news. The wagon of lumber has just arrived. We can start work on Sam's house tomorrow morning."

Jed and Ben had planned to leave in the morning, but after that announcement, it would be rude to leave. It was the way of the settlers to help each other as much as possible. Ben and Jed were ready at sun up, along with lots of other men from the lumber camp and by late evening the house was closed in, with two windows and a door that opened to the area behind the house. A second door would open into the back of the store making it easy for Helen to care for her children and still know when a customer entered the store. Jed had asked Beth to take advantage of the time to rest. She helped Gentle Fawn with the twins and took a nap in the afternoon.

The Reverend had not been there in the morning to help with the building. He had gone hunting and provided a large deer. It was roasting over a community fire. The wives from the camp of the lumbermen had been busy cooking and the wonderful aroma of the feast filled the air.

They had much to celebrate. Gentle Fawn's babies were healthy twins, and now the house was attached to the store, closed in and ready for Sam to finish inside as time allowed.

When everything was ready, everyone gathered near the fire and joined hands. Reverend Brown prayed.

"Father, we ask that you bless these beautiful babies. We thank you that they are both healthy and strong. We thank you that their mother and father are blessed. They have named this boy Stormy but with their permission I would like to add the name John. Let him be known as Stormy John Carter and this girl has been given many names. She is Anne Helen Elizabeth Carter." Applause broke out and interrupted his prayer. He paused and then continued. "Please watch over them as they grow." He recorded their full names in his book. No one spoke. He prayed for a blessing on the growing community and on their friends that planned to leave soon. "We thank you that your hand guided them on their journey so that they found Elizabeth Ann Wilson. I record her name here also as a new member of our community. Thank You for saving her from the devil's hand of destruction," he said dramatically. "We ask that you continue to bless her with strength and health. Father, we all ask your blessings on this food and on our lives as we work, live and travel. I too, will be leaving," he announced. "I will be heading south to finish my circuit during winter, but I plan to be back next spring. Now ladies, if you are ready, we can enjoy this wonderful food you have prepared for us."

Jed was shattered by the sudden awareness that the Reverend wouldn't be there. He hadn't realized that like most preachers of the day, Reverend Brown traveled a circuit.

The meal was delicious and the good friends enjoyed the company, telling stories and singing songs into the night. Jed finally got up his nerve and took Beth's hand and led her into the trees near their tent.

"We need to talk, Beth." He said. "I want; I mean we want you to come with us. We haven't a nice house like these, but it is cozy and warm and we plan on building on to it. We have a garden planted, if the animals haven't eaten it all, and we already have lots of dried meat, and I am a good hunter. You will always have plenty to eat. Come with us Beth."

"Are you asking me to marry you?" Jed was shocked! She had understood what he was saying, but was having fun at his expense.

"Yes, No, I mean I do love you Beth and I can't stand the thought of you staying here and Ben wants you to come, too. You will come won't you?"

"Are you asking me to marry you?" This time she was serious. She did love Jed, and had been sick inside at the thought of him leaving.

"Yes, I'm asking you to marry me! Here and now! We have all we need. A preacher, good food and friends and I love you Beth more than I can ever say."

"Yes Jed," was all she could answer. She had tears flowing down her cheeks. She buried her face in his shirt. She would never be alone again. He loved her! This is a miracle, she thought.

Jed let out such a whoop that it startled her. He grabbed her hand and ran into the circle of light from the fire, and said loudly, "We are getting married! Beth said yes!"

"What?" said Ben? He hadn't been ready for this. It changed everything! He was happy for them of course, but if they were married, it meant that he would just be the kid that hung around.

It was his place! It was all he had. He had worked hard to create it. He had wanted it to be three good friends. He was kicking himself for not seeing it coming. Jed walked over and put his arm around Ben's shoulder.

"Aren't you going to congratulate us, little brother?"

"You didn't say you were going to ask her to marry you! You could have told me!"

"I didn't plan it Ben, it just happened. I love her and she loves me. You said she could come with us for the summer. It is better if she comes as my wife. If we can stay with you until I get a house built, it will help a lot. We can pick a place for my house together. I always want to live near you, Ben."

Ben let out his breath. He didn't realize that he had been holding it. Ben hugged Jed and laughed loudly.

"Of course I am happy for you and for Beth, too. Beth will be a good wife for you. She is a wonderful person."

Everyone gathered around, smiling, shaking his hand and slapping Jed's back. The Reverend quietly slipped over to Beth and asked her when she wanted the ceremony.

"I must be away pretty soon so I can head south before the winter weather sets in," he said.

"May I let you know in the morning?"

"Of course," he answered. "God bless you, dear child."

She smiled and turned to be wrapped in the arms of one woman after another. They pulled her into the house.

"We have a wedding dress to make and things to get ready," said Rose, the lady that lived in the last house in the row. She would be the teacher in a few years, when there were children old enough to need one.

"We should have the ceremony in my backyard. I will open the back window wide and then we can use the piano for music. There are lots of beautiful wild flowers back there and we can gather more. We should send the men hunting. They just get in the way, anyway. She didn't wait for any comments.

Beth's mind was overwhelmed with the sudden plans.

"We will need a big oven to bake a cake. Gentle Fawn will let us use hers," said Helen. "I have a bolt of white cotton in the Trading Post. It isn't fancy fabric, but if we add lace it will be beautiful," volunteered Helen.

"Wait, please, everyone wait. I can't pay for any of this. I haven't any money," said Beth.

"We don't want you to pay for any of it. We are your friends and hope you will always be ours. We are having more fun than we have had for a long time! Now no more of that!" said Rose.

"There is a new sewing machine in the back of the store that we can use to make the dress. If we do that tomorrow, we can cook and gather the flowers the next day. What do you think, Beth? How does this all sound, to you?" asked Helen.

"Yes. Yes, of course! It all sounds wonderful."

"Let's go over to the store," said Helen.

The women went to see the fabric and the new sewing machine. None of them had ever used such a machine, but they were sure that it would speed up the process of dress making like a miracle. They all wandered into the closed-in backroom, which would become three rooms, when Sam had finished the inside. "If it decides to rain we can come in here," said Helen. "For now let's all go back to see Gentle Fawn and let her know what is planned so far."

Beth had never felt so important in her life. She was manicured, washed, curled and in general, just plain pampered. The women all had a turn on the sewing machine and each in turn made a vow to own one someday.

Rose laughed as she began her turn at sewing a seam in the dress.

"It is hard to remember to peddle with my feet and hold the material straight and start the wheel going all at the same time!"

The dress was fitted, shortened, hemmed, embroidered and embellished with handmade hairpin lace around the neck and sleeves. It was perfect. They had talked and laughed and worked, having a wonderful time. By the end of the day the ladies were pleased with the finished dress. They joined hands and each in turn prayed for a special blessing for Beth and Jed and their life together.

Tears escaped Beth's eyes. She had never known people like these.

"Now," said Rose, "It is time we all got back to our men and feed them and get some rest. Tomorrow will be a big day." The Reverend appreciated the efficiency that the ladies had used in getting ready in just two days.

The weather was warm and sunny. The men dug a pit and lined it with stones. They had surprised everyone with a fat buffalo calf to roast for the celebration. They had found a small herd that had gotten separated from the larger ones. The fire would be built in the pit and kept going all night. In the morning the calf would be lowered into the heated pit and it would be kept covered until the meat was cooked and tender.

The cake was a yellow cake with nuts and raisins in it. It was coated with a pink, sugar glaze. The pale pink color came from a few dried beets that Helen had in the store. Each woman spent hours preparing her best dishes in large quantities. Helen took time to bring a pan of warm water to Gentle Fawn and helped her to freshen up. She would be able to sit in the fresh air and attend the wedding ceremony, but then she would have to rest and her meal would be brought to her. She was still regaining her strength and learning to take care of two babies.

The twins were good babies, and as long as they were fed and dry, they didn't demand a lot of attention. Through her window, she could hear Rose practicing the wedding march. It was exciting!

In two hours, Beth would be married. It will be so quiet after they leave, thought Gentle Fawn. I wish they were building a house here. Someday this will be a town, with a church and a school. I hope they will be as happy as I have been with Tom she thought, as she drifted off to sleep for a short nap.

*****

Jed had been talking to Sam for several minutes. They walked together into the store.

"Sam, are you sure you don't mind waiting? It may be next summer before I make it back."

"Jed your craftsmanship is worth waiting for. That cradle is the most beautiful piece of furniture I have ever seen. If you make one for me to sell, it will more than pay for that simple gold band."

"It's a deal, Sam. Thanks a lot." Jed fingered the ring in his pocket. He hoped it would fit her tiny finger. Even when she does get all her weight back, she will still be small, he thought. He wrapped the ring with white yarn and tied it. There that makes it a little smaller. She can always wrap it herself with something if she needs to make it even smaller.

He walked out to see Ginger, and took her to the water's edge. She had not been forgotten. There were many horses in the settlement, but as people passed the area, she had been patted or scratched. Everyone knew the amazing story of how Ben had rescued her as a foal from the mud bog and they agreed that she was special.

Stump was enjoying the hustle and bustle. The women thought it fun to slip him special treats when no one was looking. As a result, by the time the meal was ready, he was not hungry. He went in the bedroom to get away from the activities outside and napped near the twin's cradles. Gentle Fawn thought that he was being protective and liked having him there.

Helen helped Beth slip the simple, white cotton dress over her head. She tucked wild daisies and a small circle made of lace in her up-swept hair. Beth looked at her reflection in a small hand held mirror and smiled.

"I wish I didn't look so tired. Everything you have done is so beautiful."

"We are not finished yet," said Helen. First a little bit of pink on your cheeks from the beet water we used for the cake and now hold this beet right on your lips for a moment. There. That's nice. I almost forgot! We should slip a new white stocking over each of your shoes. See? That completes the look! You are beautiful!"

"Helen, you have been so kind and generous. Thank you so much. I will never forget this day. You are all so special to me."

When all was ready, Tom escorted Gentle Fawn to a chair that had been placed in the yard for her. Beth had asked Helen to stand beside her and Ben was standing beside Jed. Rose started the music. First Helen came and stood in front of the Reverend. Then as the music started over, Beth came hesitantly. The first sight of her caused Jed's heart to skip a beat. She looked more like a small angel than a woman. Her hair was in curls around her face and she wore a crown of flowers and lace. It seemed that even the birds and animals of the forest had stopped in awe.

The sun was near setting. It created a golden glow on the small assembly as the couple said their simple vows. Jed placed the gold band on Beth's finger and saw that it would need more yarn on it to make it fit. The ceremony was brief but so beautiful that it would live in the memory of everyone there.

Reverend Brown made another entry in his book and after signatures, he handed Jed the signed marriage certificate.

Congratulations were started by a big bear hug for Jed and then a gentler version for Beth, before Tom took Gentle Fawn back to the three sleeping babies. Abe had cooperated by taking his nap a little later than usual and hadn't made a sound.

"She is so beautiful, isn't she Tom?" asked Gentle Fawn.

"Yes, she is, but not as beautiful as you." He kissed her on the cheek and told her to rest until the babies disturbed her. "Just call out the window when they start waking up and help will come."

A little later Beth changed into the leather dress that she had worn on the trail. She would not take a chance on getting a mark on the beautiful gown but she left the lace and flowers in her hair. She carefully folded the wedding dress and took it to Helen.

"Will you do something more for me?" she asked. "I would like you to put this in your store and sell it. Put the money in a fund to help the next people that come along that need it. I have all that I need," she said, as she looked down at the thin gold wedding band on her finger.

"Are you sure that's what you want?"

"Yes, I'm sure," Beth, answered. Helen carried the dress carefully to the store, smiling, and hung it up. She is as sweet as she could be, she thought.

The feast was ready. The men were uncovering the calf and putting some of the tender meat on big platters. It had roasted long and slow in the pit they had made for it.

"Every family will have meat to take home, and Reverend Brown and our friends will be well fed as they travel," said Tom.

The lumbermen and their families were jolly people, laughing and enjoying the celebration and fellowship. Reverend Brown offered thanks and prayed a blessing on the food and all the people gathered there.

After he had eaten, Ben slipped away from the party and scooped up his sleeping furs. He carried them to the tall grass behind the store, where he made a cozy nest. He checked on Ginger and brought her closer. He knew that Stump would find him when he was ready.

Ben could not sleep. He looked up at the stars and the sliver of the moon and praised God for the magnificence He had created. Then he prayed for a love to enter his life when he was ready; someone as special as Beth. He hadn't thought of such a request until today, when he saw how Jed and Beth looked at each other. He was fine until he remembered the line, "until death do us part." It made him sad. Nothing is ever certain. No one knows what the future will bring. That is, no one but God. Ben was comfortable talking to God. He had been his only companion in the beginning.

For once, Jed did not get up early. Ben had taken his axe into the woods and returned with two long poles. He was busy fashioning a Travois big enough to be pulled by Ginger. He had traded his carved cross and bone knife for the hide from the young buffalo calf and some rope. He had scraped the hide and left it by the hot pit all night.

Although it was not properly processed, the smoke would preserve it for now and he planned to rework it once he was home. It was getting stiff and would be even harder to work with if he waited. He fastened the hide to the poles hair side up with the rope. The underside was thickly coated with cooking fat. Sam had provided him with more fat in a small pouch for use during their trip home. The ends of the poles would take most of the wear, but Ben knew that occasionally the grass or dirt would scrub against the hide.

Sam had liked the carved bone knife and had given Ben enough trade credit to also get a small mirror for Beth as a gift. Ben had it hidden in his pack and wanted to surprise her with it later at the hut.

Jed came to see what Ben was working on. Ben explained what he had in mind and Jed helped fashion a pull strap that went across Ginger's chest and another around her belly, to even the load and add stability. Two more went from her chest strap and attached to the one that went around her middle.

"Once she gets used to it, she won't even feel like she has a load at all," said Jed. "I could pull this if I had to."

"Well, I did pull one with all my gear and Ginger on it when I found her. She was so weak and little that I just couldn't figure out another way to get her and my stuff back to the Hickory. I needed to get away from the mud bog and gather grain to feed her and let her rest. We camped on the bank of the Hickory for three days while she recuperated and learned to trust me and to eat soft mash.

"I thought it was a good idea to leave Ginger's back available in case Beth needs to ride. She is well now, but still not as strong as she should be."

"Thanks Ben, for being thoughtful and for everything. I owe you so much."

"Jed, that's what families do, they help each other."

They had packed up their camp so often that it took only a few minutes. The Reverend had said his good-byes, the night before. He had headed out at daybreak.

They still had a little jerky and a large section of their travel food. Jed took his firebox to the community fire and found a glowing coal. He fed it a bit and tied it on the side along with a bundle of oak twigs. The water bags were on top. Beth hurried away to see Gentle Fawn one last time and kiss the babies. She had said all of her goodbyes.

Helen brought her a small package and instructed her not to open it until she got home. Rose brought wrapped bundles of the buffalo meat, a loaf of fresh baked brown bread and some wedding cake. Sam brought out a bundle containing flour, coffee, salt and sugar.

Tom gave everyone big bear hugs and told Jed that he and Beth didn't have to wait to visit until he had his house built and that cradle made. He kidded Ben saying that he should stop by to check once in a while.

"You never know when a pretty lady might show up for you, we enjoyed having you here," he said.

Just before they left, Tom stepped around the side of his house and came back with a small wooden crate with a rooster and two hens.

"This is from Gentle Fawn. She wanted you to have them. Keep the wolves and fox away and you will have more by next year. This is a bag of cracked corn to feed them along the way." Beth's face lit up.

"I'll take good care of them and keep them safe. Thank you so much. Thank you everyone for everything," she said.

They headed back up the Silver River, the way they had come. It wasn't hard to get Ginger to pull the travois, with Jed on one side and Ben with his arm around her neck, on the other.

"Let's go Ginger," said Ben and they started out slowly. As soon as she felt the tug of the travois, she stopped. She was confused. This was something new to her. Jed gave the command again and pulled a little on the rope. She took two hesitant steps and then another. She flicked her head back to see what was holding her back, but soon was in stride and realized that it was what they expected. The new game took less effort than carrying the weight on her back. Once it was moving it was very easy. She nodded her head up and down in pace with her steps. She was happy to be moving again. Ben praised her and scratched her ears and told her she was his best girl.

Stump romped around and sailed completely over the travois. Like Ginger, he was delighted to be back on the trail.

CHAPTER FIVE   THE TRAIL HOME

"We are making good time," said Ben. By early afternoon of the next day, they were looking at the spot used by the wagon trains, to cross the river. Actually they had been moving slowly and stopping often, not wanting to tax Beth's small reserve of strength. She was determined to walk and prove that she was healthy.

With only one brief rain since they had initially crossed the Silver River, the water was lower. Jed and Ben cut four fat branches the length of the travois poles and slipped them under it and lashed them to the bottom of the travois to make it possible to float it across. The river was more manageable this time. The weather had cooperated and they knew now what to expect from this river. They took Ginger across first, with both of them swimming on the down side to guide her.

"That worked well. She didn't have time to worry about it. Now she can graze and calm down while we get the rest of the stuff across," said Ben.

Stump jumped in and paddled his way to the other side. He barked with victory, shaking water over both of them and jumping up on Ben.

"I don't think the water bothers him at all," said Jed. They looked back and saw Beth wave. She was sitting on a rock next to the make shift raft. They had asked her to remain there until they came back for the raft.

"She is a miracle, Ben. I never dreamed I would have someone like her," said Jed.

"I just hope she isn't disappointed with the hut." Ben still didn't realize that the differences he was worrying about were the very things that made the hut feel cozy and secure.

"Don't worry. She won't be disappointed. The hut will make her feel safe," said Jed, as he started to edge toward the water with a big grin on his face.

They ran into the cold water and the undeclared race was on. Jed came out a fraction of a second before Ben.

"See I told you I was a better swimmer," he said, and they all laughed.

Beth said she would swim across and they both said she wouldn't and helped her to climb on top of the bundles on the raft.

"It may tip a little in the current, so grip this rope with one hand and steady the cage of chickens with the other," said Jed, as they eased the bobbing raft into deeper water. Once again both of them swam on the down-stream side of the raft. Stump let out a howl of happiness when they reached the bank beside him. Ginger blew a greeting and hung her head over Ben's shoulder. She would always think of him as her security.

Seeing the far stretching grass of the prairie was a pleasure after the time walking parallel to the mud flats. Summer flowers grew, peeking up to display their variety of lovely colors among the many different kinds of grasses. Beth rubbed Ginger with handfuls of dry grass, while Jed and Ben stood behind bushes, and once again changed from their worn cloth trousers to the soft leather they normally wore.

"My old trousers are really getting small but they were good to swim in," said Ben as he gladly put his leather shirt over his head. "That water feels like it is coming straight off of an ice field."

They removed the extra logs used to float the travois, knowing that they could use the raft waiting for them, when they got to the crossing on the Hickory at home.

They were soon on their way again. Beth was tired of traveling and longed to be someplace with a roof over her head that she could call home.

When it was time to move out, Ben folded the quilt and put it over Ginger's back. Jed simply picked Beth up and placed her on it. She didn't get a chance to debate it. She was trying to be strong, but they could see that she was terribly tired. Ginger didn't seem to notice the small amount of weight on her back.

"Thank you, Ginger," said Beth, leaning forward and snuggling near her ears so she could scratch and whisper to her.

By late afternoon, they were traveling beside the blackened roots of the prairie fire. The grass had grown up over it, rich and green, but blackened spots could still be seen.

"Let's keep going until we get past the path of the fire," said Ben. "We can make camp in the tall grass tonight."

"Sounds good to me," Beth answered. Tomorrow we will be at the wagon train." She said it casually, but the remembered horror of the attack, was written on her face.

"If you would rather not go there, we can cut across," said Jed. "I know that Ben will not object".

"It will be all right," she said, "I just have to face it and put that part of my life behind me. Besides, I think that with a little work, the plow might still be useable. There might be other things that we can salvage, too." The idea of a plow lightened the mood.

"We sure could use that when it is time to plant a garden again. It was hard work spading up the sod," said Ben.

That night they slept in head high grass. It formed a wall around them, and made Jed very uneasy. It was impossible to see even a few feet away. He worried about predators attacking them as they slept. Then he felt concern for Ginger's safety. She gave them total trust. He didn't want anything to happen to her. He tied her to a pack as close to them as he could. Stump bounded here and there and acted as if this was a playground just for him. He flushed two birds. The ground was too overgrown with grass to light even a small fire. They ate some buffalo meat and bread and then finished with wedding cake.

They had filled the water bags when they crossed the Silver, knowing that this part of the journey was away from a water source.

Ginger had a long drink from the water that Ben poured into the big pan and so did Stump.

Ben tromped down a small circle and spread out his bedding a few feet away, leaving a wall of standing grass between his bed and the newlyweds. He heard Jed's softly spoken prayer for protection for all of them. He had thanked the Lord for the safety He provided and for giving him a family at last. Ben thought that he was glad to have a sister again, and someday he knew that he would find Sarah and then he would have two sisters.

Stump had no reservations about diving through the screen of standing grass and as everyone settled down, he took advantage of it and licked faces and wanted to play. Beth's giggle at the dog's attempt at affection put a smile on both Ben and Jed's faces.

Ben called Stump to his side and he soon adjusted his mood to the quiet camp. Ben couldn't help noticing that his leg still ached from his injury when Stump tried to put his head on it. Instead, Ben wrapped his arm around the big dog's neck and they went to sleep, side by side. The extra days at the settlement had given Ben time to start healing.

Jed lay awake far into the night, listening to the sounds in the tall grass.

The sky was cloud covered when they rolled up the bedding and prepared to move on. The wind whipped the grass and made loud rustling sounds. Jed grew tenser with each minute that passed.

"We need to get going," he said. "This weather feels weird to me. I think we are in for a really bad storm."

Back on the trail, they hurried for the tiny dots in the distance where the burned wagons might offer some cover from the approaching storm.

The first drops of rain were cold and wind driven. Jed wrapped a deerskin over Beth and they continued on as fast as they could. She could remember the condition of the wagons and didn't hold much hope for cover, but said nothing as they made their way through the rain.

It was apparent that at least one wagon train had come this way since the raid. She wondered what they thought and felt as they rolled by.

The first wagon was less than a shell. The timbers that formed its frame were burned through. The second was like the first, but the third wagon lay on its side and the flames had consumed the canvas and contents but had only scorched the wooden floor. They huddled against it with the tent propped over their heads. Ginger stood with her head under it and backside out.

"She is frightened by the thunder," said Beth. "She wants to see you, Ben and be near you."

They turned the travois over and covered the bundles and packs. The buffalo hide formed a shield. They huddled there until after dark. Finally the rain stopped. The night was so black that they could not see to move around. Jed felt under the buffalo hide for the oak twigs and the firebox. He didn't feel warmth inside until he lifted the lid. He carefully added a little twig and waited. He had a tiny glow. He added another. He wanted a fire tonight more than ever. It was growing cold and he could feel Beth shivering. He added more twigs and finally he had a small flame in the bottom of the box. He wondered where he could find dry wood.

Ben saved the day when he pulled two branches from beneath the packs.

"They are from the area where we made the raft. The wood was different and soft. I thought it would be good to carve, so I stuffed these under the packs. It's not much, but maybe we can get warmed up a little." They pulled out a patch of soggy grass until they had a circle of bare dirt and carefully transferred their fire to the ground and added more twigs and then pieces from the two branches.

Jed made a torch by splitting a piece of charred plank from the wagon. He wrapped it with the stems of the tall wet grass, tying them on with hide strips. He held it by the small fire to dry it. After rubbing it with grease, he lit it. He hurried into the night with his improvised torch.

He had seen the small rise, before the sky had darkened. If he could get near it, there were a few stunted trees. His torch was flickering. He hurried. Just then, he stumbled and fell forward. His torch slammed down hard, landing in the wet grass and sputtered out. He was a long way from the wagons.

The very small fire that marked their camp was just a dot of light in the velvet blackness.

"Father, forgive me for not calling on you sooner. I always seem to think that I can solve everything myself. Help me to find something dry to keep the fire going. Help me to take good care of Beth." He stayed face down on the wet grass for just a moment longer. He could hear the wind whistling and it made a different sound as it pushed against something. He was near the rise. He cautiously felt around before standing. He could feel pine needles. They pricked his palms. He swung his arms up and around. His fingertips touched a branch. He was beside a small pine tree.

"Thank you, Father," he whispered. He crawled under the tree, filling his pockets with the dry needles near the trunk, then he pulled the under branches off, snapping and breaking the dead wood until his arms were full. He backed out from under the tree and looked for the tiny dot of light to guide him. He could see a small glow of yellow, in the blackness.

"Father, you are my guiding light. Help me to always remember that."

He forced his steps to be cautious and sure. By the time he returned, the fire was just a small glow. He pulled the dry needles from his pockets and sprinkled them on the coals. His companions cheered as they ignited and he carefully fed the flames with the pine branches he had carried.

Ben searched in the packs and brought out the travel food. He handed it to Jed, continuing to search until he brought his hands out full of grain. He held it out to Ginger. She always appreciated grain even though the prairie was rich with all kinds of food for her. She stood near the fire, knowing that it offered protection in the dark night. Ben had pulled out another skin and they were able to sit on it and pull the tent around their backs. They were finally warm and getting dry. They munched the travel cakes and were satisfied with their small comforts.

Ben added the last branch as dawn crept over the horizon. Beth slept against Jed's chest. Ben leaned his head back against the wagon and closed his eyes.

When he opened his eyes again, the sun was shining and the morning held the promise of a beautiful day.

"Hey sleepy heads," Ben said, "Let's get things spread out so they can dry. After that, we need to do some exploring." Beth yawned and snuggled closer to Jed, not wanting to leave her cozy cocoon. Jed tickled her and slid away. He stood up and stretched the stiffness from his limbs.

CHAPTER SIX   A WOMAN'S TOUCH

There was nothing left of the fourth or fifth wagons, but the sixth had also turned on its side, a short distance from the trail. The driver must have tried to pull away. It was partially burned. Its contents still lay on the sod of the prairie, a box of ruined books, broken dishes, rotting clothes and bedding jumbled together in the grass with a broken rocking chair, telling their tale.

Ben saw that the bedding partially covered a long wooden crate. It was still intact. He used his knife to pry off the lid. Inside were three rifles and boxes of cartridges.

"If the Indians had noticed those, they surely wouldn't be here!" said Jed, as he walked up.

"The cloth they are wrapped in is soaked in oil. It is stained, but still strong. Let's take that." Ben picked up one of the guns and looked at it, seeing his father's rifle in his memory.

"This isn't even rusted," he said. He carried one of the guns in his left hand. It was indeed a treasure. "All we need to do is clean and load them."

They found pots and pans and silverware that were blackened, but when Jed rubbed a spoon with a little dirt, it began to shine.

"We will be eating like kings," he joked trying to lighten the feeling that they were standing in a graveyard.

Beth walked up and slipped her hand into Jed's.

"The next wagon was mine," she said. It was badly burned. They had all given up the idea of finding a good plow when Beth pointed at the pile in the middle of all the burned rubble.

"Look there," she suggested. Ben pushed at it and saw that buried in the tangle of debris was the plow. Its wooden handles were gone but the rest of it would be salvageable. It was a struggle to free it from the charred wagon, but once it was pulled out into the grass and brushed clean of most of the ash it looked repairable.

"It is rusty, but we can clean it up with sand," said Ben. "It should be simple to make new handles."

Jed handed the silver spoon to Beth. He could see that the sight of her wagon was taking a terrible toll on her. She had walked to the other side of the trail and stood at a pile of rocks. He instinctively knew that was where she had struggled to bury her husband by digging a grave with a cooking spoon.

"I made a pile back there of pans and more silverware. Would you look at them and see what you think is useable?" She turned slowly and moved in the direction he had pointed. It was apparent to both men, that in her mind, she was remembering the day she had to run from this wagon to save her life.

Ben and Jed continued up the line of wagons, not speaking and not finding anything else that they needed to selvage.

They did not see the simple strand of wool that Beth pulled up over her head, holding it tightly in her clenched hand for just an instant. The silver band was warm as she touched it to her lips.

"Goodbye my love. Goodbye James. I will always love and remember you," she said, as she tossed it into the rubble of their wagon.

Ben and Jed turned and went back to where Beth stood. Tears and black smudges stained her face as she stood with her back to the line of wagons and the painful memories they held.

Bravely she picked up a stack she had made of large and small cooking pots and in the top one; she had collected all the silverware she could find. In with the silverware was a small, silver, baby's cup.

"Can we pack up and leave here soon?" She asked. "I don't want to stay here any longer."

"Yes we are ready to leave," said Ben.

"I will bring Ginger with the travois and see what we need to do to take the plow home." He hurried back along the row of burned wagons.

They reinforced the bottom of the travois with more rope and a cross brace before putting the plow on it. The buffalo hide; ropes and brace were coated underneath with a thick layer of cooking grease on the bottom. This would preserve it and help Ginger to slide it through the grass. Their bedding and the tent were made into a bulky roll and put on Ginger's back.

Ben and Jed each had a big backpack to carry. The wooden crate of rifles was loaded on the travois with the plow and the chickens, as they started out walking toward the Hickory and home.

Beth walked with a stride to set a pace for the men. It seemed she was driven. After a short while, Ben insisted they stop. He said he wanted to give Ginger a break. He and Jed were really more concerned about Beth. They gave Ginger the last of her grain and they all had a drink. They nibbled some travel cakes as they headed out, this time, deliberately setting a slower pace.

It was open prairie all the way to the river. The grass was of a different variety now and the journey was easier. The sun was low in the sky when they transferred the travois to the raft.

"The Hickory appears muddy from the recent storm but not any higher than usual," said Ben.

"Since Ginger is getting better at crossing, we should leave the bundle on her back. It is up high enough to stay dry," suggested Jed. "Let's take her across first."

"If we attach a rope to the raft; we can pull it across as we go with Ginger. That will save us a trip across."

With Beth and the chickens beside the plow, Ben pulled the raft slowly across, while Jed swam alongside and kept it steady. They hooked the travois back to Ginger, and placed the raft where it was hidden in its usual place in the bushes. It was starting to get dark.

"How many more days before we arrive," asked Beth?

"Woman, you are home!" announced Jed. He picked her up and swung her around. She laughed and looked around. She still couldn't see a house.

"Where is it?"

"There," he said as the men laughed.

"I guess I did a pretty good job of hiding it from the river," said Ben. He was proud of his place. It wasn't a log cabin, but it felt so good to come back to his hut. Ben led the way around the side to Ginger's big door. As soon as he swung it open she tried to walk in, with her bundle and travois.

"I think we better unhook her before she wrecks the place," Jed said laughing. They unfastened the bundle and set it on the ground. The straps to the travois were released from her chest and belly and she trotted into her area and let out a loud whinny.

"I think she is glad to be home, too," said Ben. She rolled in the new hay in her bed and began to chew it.

"Now it is our turn, but it is dark inside. Wait here just a minute." Ben opened the split door and walked through to the front door and opened it wide. He continued on to the packs and pulled out the firebox. It was warm. He tipped the coal onto the kindling they had prepared before they left.

A new fire greeted Beth as she walked into their home.

"It's wonderful! Thank you Jesus," she said softly. "Oh Ben, how long have you been here?" "Not long," he answered, as he lit the candle and smiled at Jed. He had not told her that he had been on the wagon that left the train the same morning that the Indians attacked. Jed started to speak and Ben shook his head slightly to indicate that the story should wait.

She looked up at the center clothes tree and said she thought it was a good idea. Jed took her hand and led her outside and down to the river.

"Look back," he said. "Ben made this place nearly invisible. Even with the fire going a person would have to know it was here, to find it." She studied the scene and agreed that it looked just like a natural hill.

"That is a protection in itself. The doors are thick. Most of the place is fireproof, because of the dirt. You should feel very safe here, Beth, safe and loved. I think if I hadn't married you, Ben would have. He loves you almost as much as I do."

Ben heard the last sentence and said "Yup." And they laughed as they carried the bundles and packs in the front door.

Ben suddenly realized that Stump had taken off. He really didn't want him down by the wolf den until they had a chance to check it out. He hadn't forgotten the big, black male wolf. When he called and Stump reappeared he felt much better.

"Come on boy, you have had a long walk today. You can check things out tomorrow."

"Let's close the outside doors until we can be sure that big male wolf isn't around," said Jed. He was thinking about that wolf, too. They closed the bottom half of the door to Ginger's area and closed the outside one. She wasn't in any hurry to leave again.

Ben decided that he would make his bed on some bundles of dried grass near Ginger. He put his bed furs down and saw how soft it was. Jed arranged his and Beth's bedding together against the back wall, showing Beth the tops of the two caches. He pulled out some of the dried duck and the last of the dried berries. Beth put on the coffee pot and he started a pan of water heating. Jed added some dried herbs with the duck, then some roots and wild onions.

"That smells good already," she said.

"I would like to let those chickens out of that cage. Do you think it would be all right?" asked Beth.

"No," said Jed, "not unless you can explain the difference to Stump between a domestic bird and a wild one."

"You're right, but I think we need to make them a pen, first thing in the morning." She sprinkled some cracked corn into the cage and watched them eat, as she poured a little water in their small water pan.

It didn't take long to brew the coffee and they sat around the fire enjoying their first night at home together. Before their meal, they bowed their heads and held hands.

"Thank You God, for bringing all of us back safely. Thank You for this hut to come back to, and the food that you have provided," prayed Ben.

"Thank You again for my beautiful wife and little brother," added Jed.

"Thank You, for rescuing me and for giving me a wonderful family and home," said Beth softly.

Ben simply added, "Amen."

"Amen," they said together. Not long after the meal was shared, they all went to bed. Stump found the chickens a form of entertainment and positioned himself so that he could watch them while he ate his meal.

Ben lay on his bed looking at the flicker of the firelight on the branches of the ceiling. Again he thanked God for bringing them back safely, and asked forgiveness for loosing track of the days and not keeping the Sundays the way he had intended. Once again he thanked God for leading them to Beth, and asked protection for Sarah. Give us blessings for the days ahead. He fell asleep before he had finished his private prayers.

It was morning. Ben had not stirred all night. Jed had cleaned and loaded one of the new rifles and placed it beside Ben. He had gone out. Beth still slept feeling cozy and secure. Ben left Ginger inside giving her a pat and some grain and water before he went out. Stump had gone out with Jed. When Ben realized it, he felt concern because of the black wolf. Jed was in the trees fastening branches together using trees for corner posts for the chicken pen.

"Good morning little brother," said Jed.

"Good morning Jed. Where is Stump?"

"I checked the den before I let him out. He took off down the path. I followed him but didn't see any of the wolves near the den. I think he has gone hunting."

"Ben, I thought we could make a nice pen for the chickens here in the edge of the trees. We will need to weave willow branches thickly across the top so they can't fly out and to prevent anything from going in. If we put that cage up off the ground and block it solid on the back and sides it will serve as a little coop for now. What do you think?" asked Jed.

"It all sounds right. What you have completed looks secure and strong enough," replied Ben, "but I think we will need to put big rocks all the way around so that it is harder for a fox or a wolf to dig in."

"You are right."

"We have two hens, but if we lose the rooster, we are out of business. We can't think about fried chicken for quite a while, as it is," he said with a chuckle. I made it so this section slides open. It fastens shut here with this cord at the top and then we slide this branch through at the bottom. You can have the honor of sprinkling some corn down and letting them loose in there, while we finish the rest," said Jed.

"I'll get some willow branches and weave them into the places in the walls where there is still too much open space," said Jed.

"Do you think the top is secure or do we need more branches?" asked Ben as they finished the last section.

"No that should do it. We don't want to make it solid. They will want the sunshine as much as possible."

"I'll start getting some rocks for around the bottom," offered Ben. "I'm glad you didn't make the pen any bigger! By the time we have carried enough rocks; our backs are going to be very tired!"

"Yes, but better safe than sorry," said Jed. "Look at how happy they are, pecking around in there. They appreciate being out of that little crate."

*****

As awareness came softly to Beth, she laid in her covers, enjoying the surroundings. It is so wonderful to wake up in a cozy bed. It is difficult to believe that I have been rescued.

A smile spread across her face as she listened to the sound of Jed and Ben working outside. She could not remember the first two days with Jed and Ben at their camp, but they had told her about it.

"Lord you have given me my heart's desires. I need nothing more. Thank you for sending Scruff to find me. Thank you for giving him back to me. Thank you for the love that is here, and for Jed and Ben. Thank you that Ben is willing to share this unique home. It feels so safe and comfortable.

Beth called out from the doorway.

"Good morning. Where are you?"

"We are over here in the trees. Come see your chickens."

"That's a good pen, you made," she said. "They sure are better off in there than they were in that little cage. You did the whole thing while I was sleeping. Thank you both for everything. You have done so much for me. I love you both."

"That's what families are for," Jed said proudly, repeating what Ben had said days earlier. It had made a lasting impression.

"Now let's all go down and see if there is anything left of our garden," said Ben. Both men carried a rifle as they headed down the trail to the lake with Beth walking between them. They stopped at the den and peeked in. it was empty. Jed had checked it earlier before letting Stump out of the hut but that big black wolf was a source of concern. They explained that last year there had been a mother wolf and her three cubs in there. They continued on to the garden where they were pleasantly surprised.

Although insects had chewed some of the leaves, the plants were growing strong and developing. They could see small green knobs on the tomato plants that would later turn into a wonderful red bounty.

"The carrots are going to be big," Ben said, as he pulled one from the row. "Look they are already a lot bigger than wild ones. The cabbage plants look like small green roses. The squash has produced several big vines and are sprawling outside the garden fence. Look at these vines," he said. "They are bigger than last years and I picked fourteen then!"

"The corn looks like it is doing fine and so does everything else," said Jed. "It must have gotten enough rain while we were gone."

"God has been growing things for a long time, without any help from humans," said Beth.

"Give us a little credit, after all we did get sunburned backs planting it," said Jed, with a hearty laugh.

"It's a wonderful garden and we will be able to dry a lot of the vegetables for winter," said Beth.

She looked at the lake and the woods beyond.

"Ben, when you finally have to build a big log home, to have room for all the children you will have; that little rise just before the woods would be a great place. You could look out at the lake and the small end of the bluff and woods."

"You're right Beth. That is a good place for a house. I'll have to keep that in mind, but I am wondering where you got all those children you are talking about. Don't you think it would be a good idea to concentrate on finding a wife first?" Ben turned and winked at Jed who was wearing a foolish grin. He had to turn away to hide his delight. She didn't know it but she had just picked the perfect place for their house.

"Well Ben, finding a wife is easy. All you need to do is let Stump go off alone again. Who knows what he may find for you."

"Just a minute, I remember him bringing a bear into camp after one of his excursions! That may not be the answer for me."

After a good laugh, they talked animatedly about the garden and all the things they wanted to do during the rest of the summer.

"Ben plans to add on a bedroom to the hut and we will be making an adobe oven."

They talked about resetting the snares and going hunting for some fresh meat. They didn't want to mention the cabin for Beth. She was distracted and they wanted to keep it that way. They set the snares and went fishing for their supper. They all needed to rest a little.

The next day, a line was drawn in the dirt to indicate where the inside of the wall on the new bedroom would be. Being a typical woman, Beth insisted that it should be a little bit bigger. Jed and Ben went to work in the woods using the crosscut saw on big limbs and using Ginger's strength to drag them back.

As night approached, the next evening, the two new walls were in place. The following day they cut more branches for the roof. Beth had given herself the job of cutting willow to weave in the openings. A layer of smaller branches was added and held in place with vines and cord. Beth suggested a layer of grass bundles to thatch the roof. They thought it was a good idea. They all cut grass and layered tight bundles. The men watched over her making sure she didn't get overly tired. Beth was excited and very enthusiastic.

Jed once again took the shovel above the hut, trying to find a place where he could tumble dirt down onto the roof, as he had when they had finished the roof of Ginger's room, but when he was unsuccessful, they started digging loads of dirt from between the trees. They shoveled it onto a make shift skid and had Ginger move it to the wall of the hut where it was tossed on top starting at the back wall formed by the bluff. After a lot of hard work it began to spill onto the ground at the end and the side. That was the look they wanted. They packed it and continued pouring the dirt until it was simply a big rolling mound, blending in with the original hut. Ben and Jed packed with their hands over every inch of it. They were all delighted by the way it looked.

"Making a house this way seems like a lot more work than just building one of logs," said Beth. "What made you decide to do it this way?"

"I didn't. I just built a shack and God dumped the dirt on top of it during a big storm. The mud and rocks slid down and completely covered it. I was scared that I wouldn't be able to get out! It was so dark in side that I couldn't see anything. I felt around and found the doorway and dug until I could reach out. Now I like having the camouflage. The dirt makes it warm in winter and cool in summer."

"You fellows know that there is no way to get in there, don't you?" Beth commented, being a bit puzzled by the whole process.

"We will cut a door in the wall tomorrow and a window with a wooden shutter, for warm days," said Ben. "You will soon have a bedroom."

That night they had rabbit stew with a few baby carrots. They didn't want to use many because they felt it was wasteful, but they really did enjoy the first taste from their garden. Beth's mind was busy as she sipped her mint tea.

"I'm glad that you made the new room with plenty of head room. We can use the ceiling for added storage. You could probably put a big cache in the far end to keep the vegetables like cabbage, beets, and carrots cool. The others like the green peppers and tomatoes should be dried and go up high in baskets where it is warmer," she said.

"She is going to keep us working all the rest of summer if we let her," laughed Jed.

"She is right though," said Ben.

"After we make the doorway and box in the window, we need to have a shooting class around here," said Jed. "I don't want one of you shooting me, or your foot off. Beth, you should never leave the hut alone. One of us should go with you until you are a good shot. Promise me." Jed said firmly. She nodded.

"I am so grateful that we found those rifles. They will help us with the hunting," said Ben.

"Not unless you learn to hit what you aim at," teased Jed.

71

Ben didn't reply. He pulled one of his counting sticks from the wall and felt bad that he hadn't done a better job of keeping track. Beth asked what it was. He explained and she said she thought they could figure out if they counted backwards. When they finished stretching their memories, they had decided that Ben and Jed had been gone nearly a month. They were not sure, but decided to agree that it was Friday, two days until Sunday.

Ben went out to Ginger's area and cleaned it thoroughly. He put down fresh dry grass for her and a pan of grain. He showed Beth where the cache of grain was so she could use some of it for the chickens when she wanted it. The chickens seemed quite content in their new pen. She checked on them often. At night they snuggled together in the coop made from the cage. She did discover that the rooster was usually very late with his cock-a-doodle-doo, because he was under the trees and had branches over the top of his pen, blocking some of the morning light.

"We really should put the chickens where they get the sun sooner," she said. "That poor rooster can't do his job properly." Ben didn't comment, but he thought that it was fine if the rooster didn't wake him at dawn. Jed naturally woke early and was up doing things when Ben got up. It was Ben's preference to stay up longer and get up a little later.

The next day, Ben and Jed went to the woods to cut pieces to use as a doorframe, and to make the window frame and shutters. They were gone quite a while. What Beth didn't know, was that they were standing on the little hill between the lake and the woods, pacing out the sides of a house for her. Jed wondered if it was going to be big enough.

"I know what you are thinking. She seems to like big rooms. I guess most women are the same on that. You should make it so that the windows are in the front part. You can add a room on each side as time goes by and then add windows in them. It can grow with your family," said Ben.

"Yes," said Jed, "that sounds like a really good plan but let's get the wood cut so we can get back. I don't like leaving her alone yet."

When they came down the trail from the woods with Ginger pulling the travois with the fresh cut wood piled on it, they could see Beth sitting against the wall of the hut with sewing in her hand.

"Isn't that a pretty sight to come back to?" asked Jed, as he hugged Beth tight. "Look at all the wood we cut. We started to saw the pieces there but then we decided we could do that here and you wouldn't have to be alone."

"I'm fine, besides I wasn't alone. Scruff, I mean Stump is here lying in the trees in the shade, watching the chickens."

"One of these days that dog is going to eat one of those chickens and you won't think it is so cute that he watches them," said Jed.

They unloaded the wood and Ginger was unfastened so she could go graze.

"She sure is a big help," commented Ben.

"I have been thinking that we should make a corral for her before next spring. Have you ever noticed a herd of horses near here?" asked Jed.

"No, why?" replied Ben.

"Well, for two reasons. One they would try hard to take her with them, and second if we could drive them into a corral, we might be able to keep a couple young ones," said Jed.

"Jed you must be kidding!" Ben was astounded. "How do you think you are going to drive a heard of wild horses?"

"I haven't figured it all out yet but there has to be a way." Ben chuckled at Jed and shook his head as he headed toward the hut.

Ben ducked into the hut, pulling things away from the right wall.

"Where do you think the door should go?" he asked, as Jed came in.

"Let's put it as close to the back as we can so that the window will light the back of the main room," answered Jed.

"That's what I thought, too." They cut in the doorway and strengthened its frame with some of the wood they had brought. The sod was pulled out in big chunks and the loose dirt was pulled out on a hide and tossed up on the roof. Cutting the hole for the window was harder, because the dirt outside crumbled away. It had not had time to turn to sod. They fastened the frame for it and then made a box that fitted against the frame. Next they made shutters that swung out, to let in air and sun on nice days. It made a world of difference to the main room. It added light and a feeling of space.

"I think this is wonderful. It makes the whole place feel open and bigger. The cache should go here for the vegetables that need to stay cool," said Beth. She drew a big rectangle on the floor near the far wall. OK I will leave you two to do that, while I see about making something for us to eat, and I want to finish the curtain for the bedroom doorway. I thought a curtain would be better than a door because it will let the heat from the fire into the bedroom. What do you think Ben?"

"It sounds good to me," he said with a grin.

She left the hut with Stump beside her. Jed watched her go and called out to her to be careful.

"She smiles a lot. I think she is happy. I just wish she would gain a little more weight."

The snares held two fat rabbits. She cleaned and cut them up, rolling the pieces in flour and put them in the big cast iron frying pan with some grease in the bottom. She picked a pan full of dandelion greens, and washed them. The pan was placed near the fire with a little water in the bottom and with a cover on tight to steam the leaves.

The material from the box of guns was stained with oil but with a lot of scrubbing she had been able to clean it enough that it was usable. She boiled it in the big pan with fresh pine needles and added a bit of the dark brown dye that Ben and Jed had made with the nut shucks. Due to the oil on it, it turned out a marbled olive green. She thought it was quite pretty. She made a simple hem on all four sides. A slim branch, made smooth by scraping away the bark, became a curtain rod and a cord was attached to the wall to use as a tie back. It looked nice and served a practical purpose.

The dirt from the cache was dragged outside and dumped on top of the new room, many times before its size met with Beth's approval. It was nearly dark when they finally declared that it was done and the last pieces of heavy wood planking, from the wagon, had been put in place to finish the lid. She stomped around on the floor and continued to brush the loose dirt from the wall near the door frame and the new vegetable cache and stomped again until it was smooth and felt clean. Then she directed the moving of the bedding. Ben told her he wanted to return his to the back wall of the main room.

"Hey little homemaker, I am starving. When are you going to feed your hungry men?" asked Jed.

"As soon as you both go take a good scrub in the river." She answered, handing him the old sheet for them to use as a towel.

"She is beginning to sound like a wife," laughed Jed, as he dove in the river.

While they were gone, she made crackers on a sizzling hot pan. The wonderful smell brought the men back with dripping hair. She laughed at them and said that she had a special treat for them for working so hard. After a simple prayer of thanks, she served the rabbit with the greens and tea with crackers and honey for desert. They all enjoyed the uplifting feeling of accomplishment and a job well done.

"Tomorrow is Sunday," said Ben.

"I think you have both earned your day of rest," responded Beth. She looked at the branch walls surrounding her and the cozy fire that painted a warm glow on the faces of the two people she loved. Spontaneously she thanked God.

"It is hard for me to believe that I am no longer lost and starving. God, You have given me all that I need, and more, a home, a husband, a brother and food and clothes and Scruff, I mean Stump, is here, too. I thought that he was dead, but he is here and alive. I will never stop thanking you, Father for all you have given me." She looked away from the fire and appeared to be looking into the past.

"Beth, what are you thinking about? You looked so far away."

"Oh, Jed, not far away at all, I am totally happy to be here."

CHAPTER SEVEN   THE BLACK WOLF

Sunday was bright and sunny. Stump left at daybreak and Ginger went out on the prairie to feed. After a quiet time of thanksgiving prayer they had a breakfast of cooked wild grains with maple syrup. Jed cracked some hickory nuts and added them to Beth's bowl. He knew she needed the nutrition.

After they finished eating, Ben suggested that they sit outside in the sunshine for a while. He brought the Bible out and they sat with their backs leaning against the slanting wall of the hut and listened as he read. He ended with another prayer of thanksgiving for their safety, and for God's provision. He had read Luke chapter 12, NIV and he acknowledged that they had all that they needed. As always, he ended his prayers with a special prayer for Sarah.

Toward evening the wind picked up and rain clouds rolled over the prairie sky. Ginger had returned and was lying in the new grass of her cleaned area sleeping. Stump came in and flopped down, and then after a few minutes he got up and went back out and down to the river for a long drink.

"He looks like he has been having fun today," observed Beth. She handed him a piece of jerky as he reentered. He took it to the bottom of Ben's bed and chewed it there.

"Remember, tomorrow will be the first shooting practice," said Jed. Ben was looking forward to it, but Beth was not. Ben had used his father's rifle and been taught how to shoot safely when he was very young. He had missed the benefit of the rifle when he realized that it had been taken. He hoped that one day he would find Sarah and his father's rifle, too. He would be able to recognize it because his father had carved a small rose on the wood of the stock. He thought that he needed to be a good shot if he would rescue Sarah someday. He sat quietly and carved a small rose into the wood stock of the rifle he had been using.

"This is for you, Father." He said quietly, as he finished carving and placed the rifle beside his bed and put his arm around Stump.

A soft rain started during the night and fell gently. The morning air was clean and clear. It was a perfect day. Beth had not been the greatest shot, but once she learned to keep her eyes open while she pulled the trigger, she actually hit near the target. She found that padding her shoulder helped, too. Ben had surprised even himself by hitting on or near the mark three times out of four. Jed shot twice and hit the mark both times. He said he wanted to save the bullets and the sound of the shots carried a long way so they agreed that was enough shooting for now.

"We should start to watch for game on the prairie. We can use the top of the bluff as a vantage point," suggested Ben. That will give us a wide field of vision.

They spent the rest of the week fishing the lake and smoke drying and salting the fish. The fish were placed in a separate stone cache built in their back wall, which was part of the bluff. They added four ducks to their supplies and three rabbits from the snares. A stack of furs was neatly placed high on a rock of the back wall. They were ready to be made into clothing when time allowed.

Evenings were fun, sitting together and talking as they worked on projects inside. Beth had practiced and with Jed's help, she had learned to weave baskets and several hung from the ceiling, waiting to be filled with the dried garden produce. Jed and Ben had spent a day making another cradle. That evening and the next, they worked at carving the headboard and foot board with lovely pictures. They sanded it carefully and rubbed it with oil. It was beautiful.

"This fall we will take this down river to the trading post, said Jed. I owe it to Sam for your wedding band."

"Yes, I know. Maybe we will be able to take some of our vegetables. I plan to save and dry the seeds of everything we harvest. We can use some of them to trade. Maybe I can get some cloth, thread and yarn. I'd like to make some clothes. I plan to make some more baskets, too. They will be something to trade."

"Beth, I wish you wouldn't work so hard. You still are not very strong," said Jed.

"Oh honestly!" she said. "You fuss over me like an old woman. I'm fine now. Really! I have been small all my life."

"Sure, Honey, but please just don't get yourself so tired out," said Jed. The next morning, he put the cradle on top of the bundles of grass in Ginger's area.

"Let's take a walk down to the garden," he suggested.

"We should take some jerky with us in case the wolves are back. I would like you to see them. The mother and cubs are not aggressive but a big black male joined them before we left. He growled at us and seemed to think that he was guarding his territory. It's a good idea to always take your gun. Stay on your guard when you go in that area."

"I will Jed, I promise. Where is Ben? I haven't seen him for quite a while," said Beth.

"I don't know, maybe he went down to the garden or the lake. Let's head down there," said Jed.

He scooped several strips of the bear jerky into his pockets and picked up his gun and handed a loaded rifle to Beth.

"I want you to get in the habit of taking that with you when you leave the hut," he said.

"Jed you worry too much. Nothing can happen to us here."

"I hope you are right, but I still want you to always carry it." He made a mental note to have Ben tell Beth about the wagon raid on his family. He followed Beth down the trail toward the garden and lake.

"Are all guns this heavy? How can I do anything when it takes both my hands to carry it?"

As they neared the clump of pine trees, they heard a deep growl. The wolves had returned and the big male had moved to stand threateningly in the middle of the trail ready to spring at Beth. He had locked his eyes on her face and there was no doubt that he meant to attack. His hair bristled as he bared his teeth.

"Beth, ease to your left slowly," Jed spoke very softly. "Don't take your eyes off of him." Jed had brought his rifle up and had it aimed between the wolf's eyes. Just then a blur of fur flashed from between the dense low boughs of the pines on the right side of the trail.

The scene before them was that of two large animals in vicious mortal combat. Stump had sensed the danger to Beth and had attacked with critical intent, using everything he had to battle the big wolf that outweighed him. They bit and snarled creating wounds with each advance. The sounds brought the female and her cubs pouring from the den. Without warning, she entered the fight and just a few seconds later it was over.

The black wolf lay still on the path. The female reached over and licked Stump's neck. His wide leather collar had protected his neck and saved his life. He limped over to Beth, holding up a bleeding front paw. He looked up at her panting. Beth knew that he had offered his life for hers. Shocked by what had just happened before her, she was trembling as she reached down and stroked Stump's head and then squatted down to examined his neck wounds and paw.

"It's all right now," his actions seemed to say. The female wolf had moved back near the mouth of the den. She was still agitated. The hair on her back stood erect and her mouth was stained red, as she rumbled at her cubs and they obediently hurried into the den. She stood guard near the entrance. Having made her choice, sadly, she was again without a mate.

In all her time surviving on her own, Beth had not seen such raw violence in nature. It left her shaken and devastated.

Ben came running with his rifle in his hands.

"What happened? What was all that snarling? I was working in the garden and I could hear it clear down there."

"Stump saved Beth from the wolf!" Jed reached into his pocket and pulled out all the jerky that he had. He placed it on the ground where he stood. His arm automatically had slipped around Beth's shoulders and he drew her closer, as he thanked God that they were all unharmed. He led her around the dead wolf and down the path to the garden. Her face was pale and her legs felt weak as she leaned against him.

"Stay near Ben, Beth. I want to go back and take the wolf pelt before it gets more damage."

"Be careful, Jed," warned Beth. "The mother wolf is very upset right now. I would rather you didn't go back near her." Beth's eyes betrayed how distraught she felt.

"Beth, are you all right?' When she told him all that had happened, Ben said that he was sorry for the female. "That's the second mate she has lost," said Ben. "She pitched in to save Stump? That says a lot for their friendship. I hope Stump is okay. I can't help but wonder if she will have pups with him, but he has shown an interest in the female cub. We call her Bold One because she was the first to come near us to take a piece of jerky." Ben continued to talk as he sat down against the garden fence to rest. He was trying to get Beth to relax. She was still shaking.

"Jed brought them jerky today," she said. "He has gone back to get the wolf hide. I hope he is careful."

"He will be. Don't be upset. Wait until you see what I have been doing. The garden is growing fast."

Ben smiled at her and told her again not to worry as he opened the garden gate.

"What would you like to work on, carrots, or corn? I have the tomatoes and cabbage done."

"Everything looks like it is doing well," she said. She was trying bravely to show an interest but her mind was filled with concern for Jed.

"It looks nice where you have pulled the weeds. Ben, what are these little plants in between the tomatoes?"

"Those are marigolds. My mother always said they keep the bugs off the tomatoes. She had all these seeds in marked little packs in the wagon. We planted every kind she had. On the end over there, those are sunflowers."

"I am afraid to ask, but Ben, what happened to your parents?" They talked as they worked at pulling the weeds.

"After a moment, Ben answered.

"We were on the wagon that pulled away from the wagon train early that morning of the attack. The Indians saw us heading for the river and somehow they were there waiting for us, hidden in the trees when we pulled up. They killed my folks and took Sarah, my little sister. She was just nine years old. I will go find her someday, when the time is right. I buried my folks under the biggest oak tree, where we crossed the river coming back. Sometimes I go over there and it seems like if I talk to them they can hear me. Do you think I am being strange to talk to them?"

"No Ben, I don't think that is strange at all. Sometimes I feel like..."

Just then, Jed walked up with the wolf skin rolled up and resting on his shoulder. "The mother and cubs are gone. So is Stump. I wanted to check his wounds but I guess that will have to wait." He put the rolled fur in the shade and joined in the weed pulling. When they had finished, the garden looked beautiful and all three discovered that they were tired and had sore backs from bending over so long.

Jed picked up the wolf skin and they all walked quickly past the den, up the path to the hut without mentioning what had happened.

*****

As soon as they got back to the hut, Beth took a piece of soft leather and the clean, old sheet and said she was going to the river to take a bath and wash her hair. She scrubbed the spots off of her leather dress and put it up on the biggest rock to dry. Beth treasured the small bar of soap that Helen had put in her little bundle. As she swam behind the screen provided by the willow trees, she watched the sun reflect in the water and thought how wonderful her life was now compared to just a few weeks earlier.

"Thank you Father," she breathed as she splashed back to the big rock where her dress was drying. The sheet was warm from the sun. She wrapped it around her and crawled up on the rock beside her dress.

As she looked across the river she could see Stump playing with the wolf cubs. So there you are, she thought. Good, the swim will have cleaned your wounds for you. She sat there for a few minutes until it grew uncomfortably warm.

After pulling her dress on she went back to the hut wondering what they should make for an evening meal. She looked in all the caches. Finally she decided that she would try to make a bear meat stew and cook the last of the squash. She had to cut away a lot of the squash. It had been kept far longer than she would have ever thought possible.

This fall I will dry some of them, so that none will waste, she thought. She walked up river, along the river's edge for just a short distance then cut back through the woods to the hut. Her arms were full of edible roots and stalks of crisp crunchy greens. These will be good to eat raw, she thought. That was the first that she noticed that she was alone, and didn't know just how long the men had been gone, or where they had gone.

Once the meal was cooking, she sat down and began to brush her hair. It was thin from the starvation she had suffered for so long. It was long and very dark brown, almost black. It looked black, when it was wet. She pulled it back and braided it, tying the end with a strip of leather. She used a knife to shorten her bangs. They had grown so long that they were getting in her eyes.

She allowed herself a moment of vanity, as she looked in the small mirror Ben had given her. She was shocked at what she saw. The harsh light of the sun revealed that her cheeks, once round and pink, were sunken. Her skin was pink from the swim and the sun from the gardening but beneath her eyes was an under-lay of gray.

If I look this bad now, I must have looked terrible when they found me. I really was close to death!

"Thank you God, for saving me. Thank you for sending Jed to me." Just then she heard the happy banter of the two men returning.

Jed had a young deer over his shoulders. He hung it in the tree and after skinning it; he went to the river to wash. He plunged in leather clothes and all. She hurried down to the water's edge with the partially dried sheet. He peeled his clothes off and scrubbed them with sand, and then he washed his hair. Like Beth he liked to sit on the warm rock to dry. He turned his clothes inside out and rubbed the seams with a smooth rock to keep them soft while they dried.

"I will be lucky if they are dry by dark. They were just so dirty I couldn't stand them any longer. I was afraid you would say you couldn't stand me either!" He said laughing. "What are you cooking woman? It smells wonderful."

"I don't know how wonderful it will be. I am trying to make a stew from the bear meat. I started it quite a while ago. I thought that if I cooked it slow and long it would get tender."

"I am sure that it will be great. I love bear meat," he said enthusiastically.

Just then one of the young hens set up a racket, rejoicing about laying her first egg.

"Well that's a welcome sound," said Beth, as they both looked toward the chicken pen. "Why didn't you tell me you were going hunting? I would have gone with you."

"We thought you would enjoy your bath more if we left you alone for a little while."

"Where did Ben go?" she asked. "He could use a bit of water on him," she said laughing.

"He is by the hut, scraping the wolf pelt and pegging out the new deer hide. He has it staked out next to that buffalo hide he has been reworking. That wolf skin will make a warm coat for you for winter."

"It is sad that he is dead. He was a beautiful animal," said Beth.

"I hope it won't bother you to wear it. I'm sorry about what happened. I should have prevented it somehow. I thought that he would be a danger to us the first time I saw him," said Jed. "He wasn't like the others. He had learned to hate humans."

Ben left the hide and headed for the river.

"I think I heard someone say that I need a swim," he said with a smile. He told Beth to cover her eyes. He put his clothes up on the rock and like Beth he scrubbed off any dirt he could see. He took two quick steps and plunged into the water, diving under.

"You can uncover your eyes now," said Jed. Beth headed back to the hut to stir the bear stew without looking toward the river. Ben made headway against the current with long, strong strokes and soon was out of sight. He turned onto his back and floated, watching a large hawk circle over the prairie. Ben's long blond hair got a good scrubbing and after wringing it, he quickly pulled it back with his strip of rabbit's fur. He pushed the water from his skin with his hands and stood between the rock and river, letting the breeze dry him.

A loud splash caught his attention as Stump dove in and paddled across the river toward him. Stump climbed out near Ben and sent a spray of water flying as he shook.

"Hey guy, I was nearly dry!" Ben said as he patted the top of Stump's head in greeting. It was the only dry spot on him. Ben pulled his clothes on and walked back to the hut through the trees, using the stones and branches put down for that purpose. They had all formed the habit of using them. Even now after they had all been to the river, not a footprint gave away their location.

He smiled to think of the work that he and Jed had accomplished in just a short time. They had entered the woods and followed the deer tracks to a low spot where she stood munching the dark green grass. One shot had brought her down. Ben was pleased that he had hit her in just the right spot. He didn't want to cause suffering. She had died instantly.

After quickly cleaning the deer, the next hour was used to cut down two trees. They left them in the woods where they had fallen. Ginger could pull them to the sight of the new cabin when the house was started. This way Beth would not have any idea of the progress they were making. If she happened to look toward the hill, it would look just the same. They had removed the limbs cleanly and many logs were ready to use. The biggest limbs would make good window or door frames.

They had hurried back with the deer not letting on that it had only taken a few minutes to hunt it.

Jed planned to see if he could get two windows, for the front at the lumberyard. Later, he would order others. He planned to have the cabin done by the end of next summer. He knew with the lake nearby and the fresh spring in the woods that water would not be a problem. They would be able to dig a well later on.

The meal of bear stew was delicious, flavored with hunger from hard work. Beth was becoming a good cook and used the available greens and herbs to flavor it.

Stump seemed unusually restless and went back outside. They found him lying near the wolf skin in the grass.

"I know he was your friend until today, Stump. Thank you buddy for watching over us," said Jed.

"Maybe we shouldn't keep that pelt around, if it is going to make Stump unhappy," said Beth.

"Let's give it a few days and see what happens," said Jed.

Ben had gone out to find Ginger. She had been acting strangely the last few days. He brought her in and brushed her and gave her grain and water. Then on impulse he closed the big door behind her and opened the half door to the main room of the hut.

"She is really fidgety," said Ben as he stepped in the main room. "It could be that wolf pelt, but tomorrow I am going to climb up on the bluff and see if there are horses in the area."

In the morning he took a couple of pieces of jerky, a water bag, his carving knife, a large bone and his rifle. Carefully he headed up the side of the bluff. It was difficult to climb with so many things in his hands. When he was half way up he saw Jed and Beth come out of the hut. He waved and they waved back. He could see Ginger. Jed had a rope on her and was leading her away from the prairie to the lake area where she would be safe while they worked in the garden.

That was a good idea, he thought, as he continued climbing. That Jed is always thinking. When he reached the top, he crawled over to the edge and looked over. It always surprised him how high up it was. He could see animals in the distance, but they were too far away to tell what they were. He watched them for a long time but they didn't seem to be coming any closer.

He picked up his knife and looked at the bone, trying to imagine what shape was hidden inside. Before he realized it, he was carving and shaping the bone without any idea what he was making. Recognition came slowly. The standing bear with paws raised seemed to have always been there, waiting to get out. The growling, open mouth seemed ready to attack.

He had no idea how long he had sat there in the sun, but when he looked down at the prairie, the animals were closer. It was easy now to tell that it was a herd of horses. There were at least fifty. The Stallion stood a short distance from the rest. He was magnificent! I would love to have him to ride, thought Ben. I wonder if we could make a blind surround.

"You have a lot of beautiful wives, big fella, hope you won't mind sharing a couple with us," He said, as he started down.

He was excited to tell what he had seen and show what he had made. The fierce, little bear awed and delighted Beth. Jed said it was clever, but was more interested in the horses. He could hardly stand the thought of waiting a whole year to try to capture some of the herd.

"There has to be a simple way to enclose them so they can't escape. Tomorrow I'll go back up to the top to take a look at the land to see where they are and where they are headed. Maybe we can do this yet!" said Ben. "We know they have been up on the prairie for two days. Won't they need to go to the river to get water soon? Maybe the river can be used in some way," suggested Ben. I know one thing for sure, that it is pretty hot out there. My face, neck and hands are burned."

"That's it," shouted Jed. All we have to do is keep them away from the water until we block off a section of it, then let them into the circle for the water and close it up!"

"Do you think we can do all that while they stand out there and wait for us? It would take several days to do what you are planning. That's if we had Ginger's help to pull the logs. I don't think she is going to be much help with them so close. She wants to go to them. I closed the door to her stall again," said Jed. They talked about it all during their meal and Beth shook her head in disbelief.

"You two, certainly take on some big projects. Is there anything you think impossible?"

"No," answered Jed, "Some things just take a lot of thought, hard work, and longer to do. If we build the circle downstream where the river isn't as wide, then the woods will provide the trees we will need and the edge of it can be included to become part of the circle. We can keep them away from water and moving that direction by making little controlled fires at regular intervals along the way, between them and the river.

"We will need to make bare spots for the fires and prepare kindling and wood at each location. If we had several fireboxes, we could easily light the fires at just the right time," suggested Ben.

"Now that we have a plan, it doesn't sound so hard. We will have to go down river at first light to choose a spot to make the surround. We will need the crosscut saw and the axe," said Jed. "Also, we will need all the rope we have."

"I think we should take Ginger," said Ben, "but let's put a sturdier rope on her than usual. We have to be sure we go far enough to give us time to build the surround. They may start moving faster, as they get nearer the water. They shouldn't get a suspicion that something isn't quite right."

"They are used to seeing a few humans in the distance and an occasional small fire near the river."

"How will you keep them from going past the surround and into the woods and then down to the river?" asked Beth.

"You and Ginger will do that. We will tie Ginger outside the back of the circle, and when they come close you will light just one small fire on the down river side of the circle, that should give them the boost they need to take the open space to get to both the water and Ginger."

"Jed, you make it all sound so easy. What can I do tomorrow?" asked Beth.

"I want you to come with us. If we all work as a team I think we can actually pull this off and that way you won't be alone. I don't want anything happening to you."

"What's to stop them from coming down to the river anywhere along here tomorrow, before you get the fires ready?" Beth chimed in.

"The stallion won't let his herd come near any area that has been recently used by humans. We will cross the river and walk the bank on that side as we go down in the morning. It would be a good idea to leave a few of our things along the way. Maybe that old hide, and the old sheet, anything like that will do."

"I'm so excited that I doubt if I will get any sleep tonight," said Ben. "Let's pray for God's help and protection as we do all this so that our efforts are successful and none of us get hurt and none of the horses do either." They prayed with joy in their voices as they ended with thanksgiving for this opportunity.

CHAPTER EIGHT   THE SURROUND

It was difficult to get to sleep. Each one in his or her mind was running the coming day's activities with all the possible outcomes. The three young people left the hut with Ginger and Stump long before sun up. They carried a large bundle on Ginger's back of jerky, the water bag, the saw, axe, rope and the firebox and pieces of slate that they used to line holes near the fire pits they created along the way. It took longer than they thought it would. They gathered kindling and dry twigs, small branches and larger ones at the sight of each planned fire.

They chose a sight for the surround, along the river just before a bend that was enclosed with trees on both sides. Temporarily, the horses would not be able to see them. They had left their scent at each fire pit, and added the dropped items on the grass in between. They used anything they could think of that might carry their scent. Ben's cloth trousers and Beth's worn out dress were also dropped along the way. They hoped it would be enough to keep the thirsty horses away from the river long enough to build the circle.

They used every inch of rope they had to fasten the barricades of branches across the river, and keep them in place. These had to be tall and appear impenetrable. Rocks were rolled against the bottom to hold the sections on the two banks in place between the living trees. Strong, leafy branches were lashed together to make the gate that they would need to quickly shut. Once all that was done, they had to wait, each person at their appointed place.

The horses would have a difficult time jumping out once they were encircled because of the pull of the water. They wouldn't be able to run fast enough. They intended to only try to keep the very youngest ones or perhaps a mare or two. They all knew it would not be possible to keep the stallion for more than a few seconds once he figured out that he was in an enclosure, if they could get him in the circle at all.

Ben doubled back and lit the first fire. It was small and intended only to notify the horses of human presence and to keep them moving down river.

The horses were still far away but they were definitely heading at an angle toward the river. He hurried down the tree line to the spot of the next small campfire. He waited in the shade until he could see the horses slowly approaching, and then lit the second fire.

During all this time Jed and Beth were scooping water over every inch of branches and rope that they had touched, hoping to let the water carry away the human scent near the circle. The wind was in their favor. It blew the spots dry quickly and spread the smoke of the small fires down along the bank of the river.

The horses continued to move slowly toward the woods and the surround. Ginger seemed to know her part and played it well. She neighed loudly, protesting the rope that held her in the trees behind the circle. She called to the herd even before Jed could see them. He had stayed in the water crouched behind the gate, so long that his fingertips were wrinkled.

Beth hid in the woods beyond the surround, behind some bushes. Both of them were down wind of the surround. She too, had been in the water until it was time to hide. They were trying hard to remove any sign of human scent in that area. Ben's heart was pounding fast with anticipation, as he lit the third small fire.

So far everything is going according to our plan, he thought.

The stallion came unhurriedly walking toward Ginger, in front of his herd. His tan coat and black mane and tail shone in the sunshine. He reared and pawed the air. He wanted her to come to him. She couldn't because she was tied securely.

He thought the fallen trees trapped her. Surely, he thought, he could find a way to bring her out of the trees and add her to his herd. Hesitantly he came forward and the herd followed. As they neared the river's edge Beth waited ready to light the fire if it was needed. He stepped boldly, into the river and screamed at Ginger to join him. She called back with equal excitement as he headed toward her.

He was in the enclosure! The mares surged forward pouring into the river to drink. A few followed him into the deeper water, but most stood on the edge looking at Ginger and watching their stallion as they drank. Ben had crept to the surround behind the herd. He crouched beside Jed. They smiled but didn't speak.

Ben's arrival was the signal, they sprang forward as Beth joined them and all three pushed to close the gate swiftly. The stallion was furious and charged at the closing gate with all the strength and speed that he had. He cleared the top of the gate without a problem! Several others turned and ran out before they could get the gate completely closed.

The stallion had not gone far, and was not about to let these humans trap any member of his herd. He charged at Ben and Jed pawing and intending to stomp and bite them. They had not considered what would happen once they got some of the horses in the circle. He screamed and brought his hooves down onto the gate trying to break through. Jed and Ben had both jumped over the fence and were in the water with the milling wild horses. They had no intention of using a weapon on a horse. They had left their rifles behind the circle in the woods by Ginger. They swam across the river, climbed out and dove into the brush behind Ginger. Beth had made an immediate retreat into the woods at the side, when she saw the anger in the huge stallion.

For the moment they were all safe and were thanking God silently that they and the horses had not been injured. They waited, watching from cover to see what he would do. He stood at the gate, pawing the riverbank.

"He will never give up this many of his herd. We need to let most of them go," said Ben.

"How do we do that?" asked Jed.

"Let's untie one small section in the middle, where they will have to swim to get out. That way we can have some control on how many we let go. It will be harder for the younger ones to reach it so when most of the adult horses get out we can close it again. It will tire the little ones just trying and that should also serve to calm them a little."

"I agree. I think it will work. It sounds like the only chance we have," said Jed. "I can't think of any other way to do it."

"I am hoping that if we do that, he will take the rest and leave," said Ben. "Let's both swim out to the second section, but keep your eye on him."

"Once the section is open, we will need to be ready to drop it back in place at the same time," said Ben. They struggled to untie the cords that tightly bound the section in place while treading water.

Ben broke off two leafy branches and handed one to Jed.

"These should work to move the little ones away from the opening."

"Good idea," said Jed, as he hurried, working to loosen the far side of the section they had chosen to open.

Ben loudly asked God for His help as he untied his side, but held it in place until Jed motioned that he was ready.

The horses were splashing, thrashing around, and calling to the stallion, and making an overexcited commotion that none of them had ever heard before.

Ben and Jed jerked the section of fence to the side and as they did an immediate surge of the trapped horses came toward the opening. Jed swung his leafy branch inside the fence and pushed at the face of a small black foal as it tried to keep up with its mother. Ben was doing the same on his side with a pretty, white one.

"Get ready to shove the fence back over to me," yelled Jed. Ben pushed up the section of fence and held it above the water all the while trying to keep afloat and push the leafy branch at the white foal. He didn't want to lose him.

"Now let's close it!" Jed yelled and Ben tossed the section up and across the opening, just in time to stop the favored foals from escaping. They tied the section of fence back in place and for added measure they wove the leafy branches they had used into that section.

It wasn't until that moment that they had time to look up to see where the stallion and the herd were. He stood pawing the ground like an angry bull, not far from the bank. He was glaring at the two men with murder in his eyes.

The herd was scattered on the prairie after their scary experience, not in the usual close formation. As the members of his herd escaped from the surround, they swam to the bank near him but once they were out of the water, they ran out on the open prairie, in different directions, driven by fear. That worried the stallion as much as the men and the strange enclosure. Things were not in order. He couldn't think about what had just happened. He had to gather his herd so he could protect and control them.

Ben looked inside the fence and was surprised to see four little ones and a mare that would deliver before long. What on earth were they thinking? How could they take care of, and feed that many horses? His thoughts were a mixture of joy and confused concern.

The stallion reared and screamed, running toward some of the mares nipping at their flanks as he overtook them. He gathered them and forced them to run in front of him. The babies called to their mothers and the mares did not want to leave them. They tried to double back, wanting to retrieve their foals, but he wouldn't allow it. His anger was as frightening to them as it was to the humans that had taken some of his herd.

The only mare left in the circle was frantic. She backed up to the gate where she had entered and let her hind hooves fly. The blow rocked the entire side of the circle. She did it again and again, pounding at the wet, fraying ropes until she stood with her feet wide apart and head down. She was totally exhausted.

The stallion had watched her defeated efforts, from a distance, then turned and headed away, gathering the mares and nipping flanks, to force them to leave their foals. He drove the herd ahead of him.

Beth came out of the woods and gave a whoop.

"I can't believe that you did it. This was the most exciting thing I have ever seen!"

"It was fun, wasn't it?" said Jed.

"You both know that the job is only started, don't you? We have got to somehow move these creatures back and fit them into Ginger's area. All of them need to be inside where he can't get them back. He may try every night for a while. Any ideas?" said Ben.

"Well, I think we should start with the littlest one and get a rope on her and tie her to Ginger," offered Beth.

"If we remove sections and push the sides of the circle in as we work, it will be easier at the last to fasten the mare," said Ben.

"She will watch and be less afraid as she sees what we are doing and that we aren't hurting the babies."

"Ben, that just might work," said Jed. "Do you think that Ginger will mind being tied to a string of babies?"

"She is usually agreeable but this has been an unsettling day for her. I'm going to go talk to her for a while and calm her down. She was trembling when all that was going on."

They watched Ben swim back across the river and saw him hug Ginger and scratch her ears and stroke her neck as he talked to her.

Jed then turned his attention to Beth.

"How are you doing with all this going on? Are you alright?" He put his arms around her and held her against his heart. She looked up at him and smiled.

"I am fine, Jed. I thank God that no one was injured by the stallion. That was frightening when he turned on you and Ben."

"I never realized how big and powerful a horse could be, but it was worth it," said Jed. "Just look at those beautiful foals. I am excited to get them home and start to gentle them," he said.

"Jed, I feel sad for them. They are so young. They still need their mothers. How will we be able to feed and care for them?"

"Ben will be able to help us with the answer to that. Remember that Ginger was very small when he rescued her."

"Let's swim over to the other side and sit with Ben and Ginger. We should all have something to eat before we start roping the horses." They walked into the water together and swam over with easy strokes. The shade of the trees felt cold on their wet skin and clothes. "Our clothes are going to really shrink if we don't get back in time to work the leather before it dries," commented Beth.

"If your dress dries on you, maybe it will shape to your girlish curves a little. That's not at all bad," said Jed. She chewed a piece of jerky with a silly smile on her face and watched the horses in the enclosure.

"I wonder what the new foal will look like. Maybe it will look like the stallion. That would be nice," Beth said. "I think he was handsome."

"I'm just concerned for the mother right now. She is really stressing. We need to get her calmed down," said Ben.

"Let's try to move the sides in enough to take out one of the sections. We can use that rope for the little black foal." They worked their way to the front of the circle and loosened the sides easing it in slowly and carefully. They never gave an opening for escape.

Once that section was out, it was an easy thing to use the rope and get near the tired little black foal to slip the rope around its neck. Ben swam with her to the loose section where Jed helped him to take her out and up the bank near Ginger, who greeted her warmly and rubbed her muzzle on her. Ben tied the rope to the one on Ginger. She was calm and was pleased to have one of her kind near her at last. Ben was relieved to see the way she greeted the baby.

"She seems to think it is a gift for her," said Ben.

He compared the size of the foals to the size Ginger was when he had first gotten her. Ginger wasn't much smaller than the black one and the white one is bigger than she was. It shouldn't be too difficult to get them to eat mash and then grass, he thought.

Next they took out one of the brown foals. There were two brown ones so much like each other that they had to be twins. Each had a darkening on their legs and a patch of white on their foreheads. They were not as large as the white one, but larger than the black.

After removing another section, the last youngster to be removed from the enclosure was the white one that Ben liked the best. He had more spirit and fought the rope at first, but was tired and finally gave in to being led up the bank with the others. Ben tied him securely to a nearby tree. The mare was now standing just knee deep in water, in the center of a triangle. The rope that had held their bundle on Ginger's back was fastened to a tree. Beth and Ben each held one corner of the triangle fence together. Jed stood and leaned in toward the mare talking to her. She was breathing heavily and looked totally spent. He gently slipped the rope over her neck and pulled it up just tight enough so that it wouldn't easily slip off. He didn't try to pull on it. Slowly the sections were removed. She didn't try to run. She edged out of the water and stood on the bank near the others with her head hanging down.

"I think she is going to foal soon!" said Beth in alarm.

"She is stressed and very tired," Ben answered. "I would like to get her to the hut before she does, but I don't think she can make it."

Just then she took a couple more steps away from the water and dropped down, rolling on her side on the ground. Jed was very concerned, but still thought it was something they could deal with if they kept their heads.

Ben took charge.

"Jed, I am going to take Ginger and Beth back to the hut, with all the foals. Beth, you should stay there and cook a huge pot of mash to feed these babies. I'll move everything out of Ginger's area and put a soft layer of dried grass on the floor, and then put Ginger and the foals in. We should keep the top half of the main room door open so they can see you. That way they will have light and you can talk to them."

Ben continued. "As soon as I can shut the big door on Ginger's area, I'll come back here. Jed, you are better equipped to stay here and try to help this mare if she should foal."

"Don't forget to take your rifle," said Jed. "I have mine if we should need them and be on the lookout for the stallion. He could come up on you suddenly."

"At least we are on the opposite side of the river, so he would have to cross to get to us." said Ben, as they started out. The mare was kicking her feet and pulling back her ears. Her eyes had a wide open, wild expression.

"Go ahead and go, so you can get back here before it's totally dark. I'll do what I can for her."

"God be with you," said Ben as he led Ginger slowly toward home, he turned and saw Jed talking to the mare, trying to calm and comfort her.

The three smaller youngsters walked along as if they had been led before. Only the white one tugged and fought against the control of the rope. He too soon walked along when he decided that it was useless to fight.

"Of all the horses I have seen today, the stallion was the only one that I thought as fine as this little white foal, said Ben. She could see that he was already fond of the spirited little fellow.

"What are you going to name him?" She asked."

"Oh, I haven't even thought about that. I want to know first that it is alright with Jed if I choose him."

"Which one do you think you would like to call yours?" he asked.

"We should probably wait to start choosing, as you said, but since you asked me, I think I will probably favor the new foal, just because it will be so tiny and a surprise." Then she said softly, "Please God let the mare and foal live. Let them be safe and well."

"Amen," said Ben. They walked at a slow pace with the frightened, tired babies. When they reached the hut, they tied Ginger's rope to the tree nearest the door to her area, and left all the little ones fastened to her. Beth and Ben worked quickly to clear the area of everything, and then spread down new dry grass from the bundles they had stacked outside. The biggest watertight basket they had was filled with water and placed against the wall. They led Ginger with the babies still attached into the space and Ben shut the big door.

He untied the foals and found that they immediately started to mill around looking for a way out of the enclosed room. None of them had ever been in a building before and felt trapped again.

"Beth, quickly get the grain for the mash out of the cache and then stay out of this area with the foals until Jed and I come back." He stood between her and the horses until the cache was secured and she was safely on the other side of the main room door. Ginger stuck her head over the door and neighed. He hugged her neck and whispered in her ear.

"Ginger you did a good job today. You will always be my favorite. I love you girl. You're such a good girl." He scratched her ears and offered her a share of the grain. She ate it, took a drink from the basket and went to her usual spot and lay down in the hay. Her peaceful attitude calmed the young ones and soon, much to Beth's relief she saw that they were settling down to rest, too.

She put the mash on to cook and as the grain began to swell she had to transfer some of it to a second big pan. She added more water and continued to let it simmer. She got out one of the scorched pans from the wagon train and scrubbed it clean and put on some water to heat. She added some deer jerky and vegetables that hung in dry strings above the fire pit.

Suddenly, she remembered the deer that Jed had hung in the tree. I wish I had used fresh meat for the stew, she thought. Hurrying outside, she tossed a handful of grain in the chicken's pen and gave them fresh water, before going back inside. She cut a large roast to put over the fire.

It will be dark soon. I hope Jed and Ben are all right, she thought. Beth sat down by the fire with her arms wrapped around her knees. She started first to hum and without even realizing it, the words came to her lips. *"We are companions on this journey, sharing bread and sharing life, and in the love we have, is the grace we share, for we believe in the one true God."*

She wrapped Ben's quilt around her shoulders for the comforting feeling of security it offered, more than warmth and sat there waiting, eager for their return.

Jed didn't really know what he could do, but he had helped with the birth of a human baby once and he thought that it shouldn't be very different. He wanted a small fire to warm some water, but he thought that the fire might make the mare panic even worse than she was. He pulled his shirt off and slowly drew it over her eyes. She lowered her head on the grass and after a while her breathing seemed less frantic. Jed searched the area for any herbs that might be helpful to calm her.

He finally made up his mind that he needed the fire more than anything. It would keep predators away and he could make a potion to ease her stress. He swam across the river in record time and hurried to the firebox. It was out.

Just as he was getting angry with himself for wasting time he saw exactly what he needed, a tiny little vine that, when crushed and steeped, would ease her distress and calm her. He grabbed great handfuls of it and thrashed the water madly with one arm getting back without losing any of the pieces of the vine. He approached her softly, not wanting to alarm her.

He pulled a bowl from his bundle, and was extremely glad that he had stuck it and a few of his medicinal herbs in the pack at the last minute. He crushed the vine into the bowl and added willow bark scrapings. He had no idea how much he would need for a large horse, but he knew that he should make it stronger than he would for a human.

After clearing an area that was down wind of the mare, he picked up two sticks that looked like the hand of an angel had set them beside him. He began to twirl the first pointed stick on the top of the flat second one. The small pile of twigs and dry grass that he had scraped together would need a quick help to keep them burning once he had a glowing coal. He worked into a sweat never letting up on the pressure and after what seemed to him, an eternity; the coal appeared and dropped onto the dry grass. A gentle blow turned it into a small flame. He coaxed it into life with twigs and more dry grass, then small branches from the near pine. He knew he would soon need the fire for light.

Ben hurried back and got there just as it was turning dark. He stayed back and quietly gathered armloads of dry branches for the fire.

When the mare's head came up abruptly, they knew it was the start of the foal's arrival. Jed had tried to pour some of the potion in her mouth, but much of it ended up on the grass. He placed his hand on her side and could feel the hard surface. Finally she put her head back down. She was able to relax for only a moment before another contraction brought her almost upright. Jed held her head and talked softly to her. Ben knelt in a position to help if he could at the proper moment.

"She is so tired. Please Father, let this go quick and easy," said Jed. He trickled a little more of the potion into her mouth. He felt relief just knowing that she had taken a little. He placed his hand on her side and could feel the surface harden and then two tiny black feet appeared, followed by a black nose. Ben wrapped his hands firmly around the feet and pulled gently. Into the world came a tiny slippery copy of the stallion. Every detail was the same.

Jed quickly reduced the fire to a small glow with sand and dirt and then removed the shirt from the mare's eyes. She nudged the baby that Ben placed near her nose. She licked him and nudged him again. The foal opened his eyes to an almost dark world.

Later, two smiling faces cheered the little guy as he struggled to stand for the first time. His mother seemed to regain her strength when she saw him. It took him only a short time to find out where he could nurse. In the excitement of the birth, both men had totally forgotten that this was a mare from a wild herd.

Now that she was recovering, and things were calming down, they were awed by what had just happened.

The little one showed no fear of them at all. The mare still shied away, but seemed to want to trust them. They brought her to the water's edge so that she could drink and they picked great armfuls of grass and put it at her feet. They searched the area and found a stand of dry grass and made a bed for her and the wobbly-legged baby farther from the water. All the while they had not even thought about the hour or their own needs.

Not until after she and the foal were both down in the hay and asleep, did they remember that they had not eaten.

After the hard work of the day they felt starved. Ben searched the bundle and found just three pieces of jerky.

"Well it won't be the first time we have shared," he said as he broke the third in half and gave Jed an equal portion.

"It will be difficult for Beth to deal with all the hungry babies. I hate leaving her there. She is probably worrying," said Jed.

"Jed, she will be fine, and think of her joy when she sees this beautiful baby boy tomorrow."

"We will have to take it very slow and then stop and let him rest often. He is so tiny. I wonder if all new born horses are this little," said Ben. They talked about the foals they had caught. Ben told how special he thought the white one was. Without realizing it, they were imprinting their voices and scent on the mare. Jed was slowly stroking her neck as they talked. She didn't seem to be bothered by it. When he finally moved his hand away, she raised her head and looked at him.

"I think she likes it when you stroke her. She looked at you when you took your hand away." Jed put his hand back on her neck and she relaxed again. "See that? She has bonded with you already. She may still be skittish for a while, but I think you have got a mare!" said Ben.

"I am worried about what we can do when we have to let the horses out to graze," said Jed. "What if the stallion comes after them?" Ben had been thinking about that, too.

"Do you think that we could build a corral using the bluff as the back wall and fence through the trees to the river, then back up to the bluff," asked Ben? If we did it so that it included the hut, we could leave the big door open and they would still have that for shelter, until we can build a barn."

"We could do it," said Jed, "but it's a cinch that you would no longer be invisible from the river."

"Jed I know what you are saying, but there has to be a way to accomplish it and still stay less noticeable."

They dozed a while and by morning the sun had dried their clothes and the fire had gone out. They stirred it and covered it with dirt and sand and poured water on it just to be sure.

Then Jed walked over to the mare and stroked her neck as he had done for so long after the arrival of the foal. He talked to her and said it was time to take her home soon. They cut the rope shorter that held the mare and used the piece to create a backpack to hold their tools and few belongings. Ben volunteered to carry it and the crosscut saw swung over his shoulder. He carried his rifle in his right hand.

With Jed leading the mare slowly, followed by her new and still unsteady, baby, they began their very slow journey home. Ben deliberately stayed back a little to be able to serve as rear guard.

104

With the foal as small as he was, he was easy prey for any large predator. They hadn't forgotten the mountain lion that had stalked them when they had been on their eventful journey to the settlement.

They stopped often and after the second stop, the foal decided he had to have a snack so they waited for him to nurse. Jed fed grass to the mare and scratched her ears.

"She is an angel, isn't she?" He said. "Can you believe that she had never been near a human before yesterday?" Ben thought that it was more likely that she was a horse that belonged to a settler and that the stallion had stolen her recently, but he didn't say it.

"That would be a good name for her," said Ben.

"What would?"

"Angel."

"She is good and gentle, isn't she?" Jed was smiling broadly. "I think you're right. Let's call her "Angel," he said. He was smiling from ear to ear as he patted the big, brown mare. He was still absorbing the fact that they had a mare and a beautiful new foal.

They continued on for a little but soon found that the baby was falling behind again.

"He is just too small to travel. I think he needs a nap, said Jed. "Do you think Angel will mind if I carry him the rest of the way?"

"If you can do it so she doesn't get upset with you, it should be all right. Go ahead and try." Jed gently picked up the foal and brought him up to Angel's muzzle so she could see that he was fine and quite happy to be getting a ride. Jed laughed at her when she came up behind him and nudged his back.

"Maybe she wants you to carry her, too," suggested Ben with a hearty laugh.

"He is a lot heavier than he looks," said Jed after a few minutes. "It is a good thing that we are almost there." As they rounded the trees and the hut came into view, Jed gently set the baby on his legs. "I want Beth to get the whole effect," he said.

"Beth, we are back. Honey, come out and see what we have," Jed called. Beth came out the front door quickly. "Oh, What a beautiful little horse; boy or girl, she asked? She got down on her knees so she could cuddle close to the baby horse.

"Boy," they both answered at once.

"Ben, he did surprise us. He looks just like the stallion. He is gorgeous! Oh I love him," she said.

"He is yours to name," said Jed.

"Can we call him Surprise? He is perfect!"

"That's a good name. Meet his mom, Angel."

"Angel? How did you pick that name?"

"We picked it because she is an angel. You will see when you have been around her a little while. She came through that whole ordeal like a hero. She has been so good and gentle and she is a good mother, too," said Jed. He put his hand on her neck and stroked it as he had done often since he had made friends with her.

"I can't understand how you got her to let you touch her that way in just one night!" said Beth in astonishment.

All of a sudden, Beth's expression changed as a feeling of being overwhelmed washed over her.

"We have some very hungry babies in there with Ginger and she wants out in the worst way. Stump has been gone since yesterday morning and I was so worried about you both gone all night trying to help the mare and the deer needs to be processed, and what are we going to do for a corral, with all these horses? The stallion could come and take them back if we can't protect them?"

Beth started to sob and couldn't stop herself. The waiting and concern mixed with first fear and then relief and joy were too much for her to deal with all at one time. Jed understood perfectly. He was feeling the same emotions, but wouldn't allow his to show. He held her close and wiped her tears from her cheeks with his thumbs.

"I have the answers for most of that at least," said Ben. "If the two of you will help me to get some mash into the foals inside as our first project, I think I have figured out a way to make a corral and water hole that won't be easily noticed from the river."

CHAPTER NINE   BUILDING A CORRAL

They tied Ginger near her big door in a patch of lush grass and put a fresh basket of water where she could reach it. They placed Angel just a few feet away and didn't bother to fasten Surprise, because they knew he would not leave his mother's side. They gave Angel a basket of water, too.

"Now on to the foals," said Ben, as he opened the front door, he was met by the white foal. "Wow! I think we have got ourselves a jumper here," he said as he pushed the foal back toward the door he had jumped. Ben opened the half door and Jed helped him to maneuver the foal the rest of the way back through.

"Can you believe that guy? He is really something. How on earth did he do that? He was trying to get out! We will have to watch him closely or we will lose him," said Ben.

"It's a good thing that I closed the front door tightly or he would have darted out," said Beth.

All the foals were circling around in the area pushing against the big door. They had seen Ginger taken out that door and wanted to go out. They were afraid of these humans and wanted their mothers and their milk.

"It isn't hard to teach them to eat the mash, if we thin it with water. The first few times might be difficult, but Ginger learned to eat it quickly," said Ben. He carried the smaller pan of soupy mash over to the black foal first. He offered his fingers as he had to Ginger. The foal didn't seem to know what he was doing. He scooped some of the mash up and rubbed it onto her lips. She licked it off. He did it again, trying to get her to follow his hand into the pan, but after a few more attempts, he could see that she was too afraid of him to trust him yet.

"Beth would you try?" He asked, stepping back. Ben handed the pan to her and bent down to scoop grain from the cache. He wanted to give some to Angel. He realized that the supply was lower than he thought. "We will need to go out on the prairie and find grain after we get the other stuff done. This won't be enough to last until we get them all weaned," he said. Ben offered a handful of grain to the white foal and he bunted some of it onto the dirt floor but accepted the rest and chewed it.

"Yea, there is a victory! He is already able to eat grain. There's a good buddy. Have a little more. Sure, there you go buddy. You are hungry, aren't you?" He slowly brought his hand up and scratched the foal's ears, first one side, then, the other and slid his hand down his neck and over his back.

"I want this one to be mine, if it is all right with you both," said Ben. "I want to call him Buddy. He is going to take a lot of work, but I know he will be worth it."

"Hey, that's fine with us," said Jed. Beth was nodding agreement as she held her fingers in the mash and watched the little black foal suck the mash from the pan. She didn't want to speak and startle her.

Jed had been working with one of the brown twins and had gotten her to accept him enough that she was seeking his mash-covered fingers. The three young people all smiled and worked to fill the empty tummies of the baby horses. They couldn't believe their eyes! Yesterday they had just one horse, Ginger. Now they had seven!

The sweetness of the moment was shattered when they heard Angel's scream. They rushed for the door. Stump had finally come home and had come bounding up in his usual, exuberant way to say hello to Ginger. He had stopped abruptly only a few feet from the new mother and she was afraid that he would hurt her baby. She was rearing and ready to bring her hooves down on Stump if he came within reach.

Ben bent down on one knee and called the dog to him. Stump wagged his tail and licked Ben's face but all the while it was apparent that his main attention was still on the new horses he saw, standing near Ginger.

Ben picked Stump up. He was a big dog and this was not something that Stump was used to having Ben do, but he decided it was a new way of his friend showing him love and attention. Ben carried him slowly over to Angel. He waited for Jed to calm her. As Ben approached the mare's face with the dog, her ears went back and she began to stomp nervously.

"Easy girl, easy, said Ben. I want you to become good friends. Stump, this is Angel and Surprise. They will be staying with us from now on. It is your job to protect them and watch out for them, the same way you have for the rest of us." He kept his voice soft and even. Trying to sooth the mare and give Stump a chance to get her scent and for Angel to smell him and see that he was not a danger to her.

Jed continued to stroke her and talk to her. Ben eased closer so they could smell each other. She blew at Stump and he jerked back, and then extended his neck again sniffing at her. Ben lowered him to the ground a few feet away and let him smell the foal in the same way. Angel eyed him critically. If he alarmed her with any fast move, he would pay for it with a hard kick. Ben knew that was something he didn't want to risk. He had been on the receiving end of a horse's hoof and never wanted to go through that pain again.

The foal was accepting. He sniffed Stump and decided that the idea of a snack was more interesting and started to nurse. They all relaxed when Stump went over under the trees to check out what the chickens were doing.

"Guess what guys," said Beth. "We have three fresh eggs. We can either have one each for breakfast, or I can bake us a real cake as soon as time allows! What will it be?" The vote for a cake was unanimous.

They returned to finish feeding the foals.

As soon as the little ones had settled contently, Beth and Jed listened to Ben's plan.

"All we need is a big enough snag here, in the river, and then we can go up river to the place where the trees grow right to the water's edge. What we cut, we can drop into the river. The water will bring them all here. All we will need to do then is pull them out and fasten them together to build our corral. For their water source, if we dig a six-inch channel and line it with rock, we can fill the shallow in the trees for a watering hole. What do you think?"

"Ben, that sounds like it will work," said Jed. "We can drop a tree here and one on the other side and fasten their top branches together in the middle of the river to make the snag. After we haul out the rest, we can use those. We can easily hide the mouth of the ditch with brush or something. Let's get started!" He was enthusiastic.

"I left the crosscut over there by the pack when we got here," said Ben as he stood up and headed in that direction.

"Wait a minute," said Beth sternly. "You haven't eaten since lunch yesterday and that was just jerky. I have a thick stew in there, hot and ready."

"You don't have to tell us twice," said Ben. He and Jed hurried to the edge of the river to wash the remnants of mash from their hands. Beth had bowls of the stew ready when they entered the hut.

"Before we do anything else, let's join hands and give our Lord thanks. Father, we thank you for the beautiful horses and the fact that we are home with all of them, safe and sound," said Ben. "And for the stew too, Lord. I am hungry!" They laughed and gobbled their food, eager to move outside and begin their project of making the corral.

"We better introduce Stump to the foals, so he doesn't jump in there and scare them." They repeated the process of introduction with each of the young horses. Like Surprise, they thought that he didn't seem harmful. Only the little black one pushed against the wall and tried to keep a distance.

"She is a shy one," said Beth. "She will take a little longer, but she will get used to him."

"That was great stew, Beth. Thanks for having it ready. Now we have to get started on the corral, it is past noon," said Ben, as he cut two large slices of meat from the roast, handing one to Jed as they went out the door. It started to rain as they cut the first tree and watched it splash into the river filled with circles from the raindrops.

"This rain isn't going to make our work any easier," commented Jed.

"Well it won't stop us. We will be in and out of the water until we have all the logs cut and pulled up from the snag anyway. It looked like it was raining yesterday, to the north of us. I'm glad it didn't come when we were trying to bring all the horses home."

"It may have been raining north of here for a couple days. I noticed a lot of mud on the legs of the wild herd when we first saw them."

"That's interesting. When I was up scouting the herd, I didn't even notice the sky in that direction, said Ben. Ignoring the light rain, they started to work. They picked a tall, skinny pine tree on either side of the river that grew almost opposite each other. The saw made quick work of it and soon the first one was bobbing recklessly on the water, with only its bottom branches holding it from taking off downstream.

The day was warm enough that the swim to cross was a pleasure. The second tree crashed into the water sending a spray high into the air. Its top smacked the top branches of the first one and for a few seconds they thought that they might lose both of them to the current. The trees bobbed uncontrollably. Jed dove in and swam to the point where the trees met. He started immediately to lash the tops of the two trees together with vines and ropes, while Ben braced the bottoms with several rocks.

Ben jogged his way up river to the site where the trees closed in on the riverbank. His heart was racing and a prayer of thanksgiving came to his lips as he chopped the trunk of the first thin pine and watched it fall into the moving water. It didn't take him long to send a second and a third on their way down stream. Jed had remained until he was sure that the snag would hold and do its job and then he joined Ben, bringing the crosscut saw. They made splash after splash. Tall thin pines would serve well as posts and cross braces.

By the time they arrived back at the site of the snagged trees, Beth had started to use Ginger to haul the trees from the water. Ginger walked up toward the bluff pulling a tree and stopped. The tree was untied and she was led back down for another. Jed and Ben set to work stripping the branches from the downed trees. With Ginger's strength, the work was made easier. They intended to cut more trees as needed from the woods that the corral encircled, but the part near the river had to be left natural.

They scrubbed the banks with branches and poured water over the sand. When they left the river, there was no sign that they had been there. Had someone inspected the woods on either side, they would have found two stumps cut close to the ground and hidden by nature. Farther up river, the stumps were visible but there was no sign of the reason or person that had cut them.

Thick cord would be needed to bind the fence of the corral together with the living trees of the woods. The thicker branches would be used to fill in and stabilize.

"We won't finish this by dark. We need to figure out what we are going to do with all the horses for tonight," worried, Jed out loud.

"I have that all figured out," said Ben. "You get to sleep with the horses!" He gave a hearty laugh, as a strange look came over Jed's face.

"Not really, but I did think that it would be a good idea if we made a long, tall section that would form a triangle with the end of your bedroom and the wall of the bluff. We could put Buddy and the two browns in it just for tonight, and then there would be room inside for Angel and Surprise, with Ginger and the little black foal."

"That wouldn't be hard to do and I doubt if the stallion would bother them," said Jed. "It's the mare and Ginger he wants. If we leave the window open we can hear if anything disturbs them.

"For a minute there I thought you intended to put some of the horses in the bedroom." Jed had listened and nodded in agreement as Ben continued.

"When we are ready, we can use that section of fence as part of the corral."

"We should probably take time to tie branches over the top after they are in for the night so that nothing can get in to harm them. I hope the rain stops by then. Oh, by the way, one of the brown foals is a female." Jed was smiling. "She is too young for him to care, but I thought you might want to know. I noticed that when I was feeding them," said Jed.

"That's great! That means that we have a better balance. We have four females and three males."

"We should probably start the section for the triangle now. So that when we have done all we can for today, it is ready. Let's prepare the branches to cover it, too. They can be there in a pile and we can just secure them on," said Jed.

Beth walked up with a smile and said she was going to pick a big fresh batch of greens to go with the deer roast, and start more mash cooking before she went back to making cords for the fence. Both men agreed that they would appreciate that a lot when they were done for the day.

While she was inside, Beth visited the foals and gave them fresh water and offered each one a little mash. She knew that the more contact they had with humans, the easier they would be to handle.

Just as she was going out the front door, Stump went racing in passed her and put his paws on the top of the door of the stall. He seemed to just want to look at all the new horses. She gave him a minute then gently ushered him back outside. After giving Ginger a hug and some good scratches, she approached the mare slowly. She had brought her a small pan of grain. At first Angel backed up, but with gentle coaxing she was able to get her to come eat the grain.

The foal looked on with interest. She knelt and scratched his ears and told him he was the most handsome boy in the world. Her thoughts were scattered as she moved from one task to another. She checked the wolf hide that had only had a little work done on it. She didn't want it to get hard. She smeared it with the grease Jed had put beside it and quickly scraped the surface to help it absorb the grease and soften.

The smell of the roast drifted over to her and she felt nausea. That's strange, she thought. I must be just over tired again.

She sat with the growing pile of cords in the shelter of the dense pines where she could watch the mare and foal. Ginger had been so good about accepting the new horses. She really is a sweet creature, she was thinking, as the men came up beside her.

"You have made a lot of cord, Beth. We will need it to stabilize the corral walls in some places. Thanks," said Jed.

Ben smiled at her.

"Good job," he said as he walked toward the hut.

"I am going to go in and feed the little ones."

"You don't need to feed them yet. I gave them a little mash just a few minutes ago, but it is good to check on them, and would you please stir the mash as you go past. Make sure I put enough water in it this time?"

"Sure, be glad to," he said.

When he came out of the hut, he had a troubled look on his face.

"The little black one doesn't seem to have much spirit. Did she eat?" He asked. "I hope she isn't sick."

"I don't know much about baby horses, but she ate for me," said Beth. "I just think she is timid. She may need more gentle attention than the others."

"Well Jed, if you can break yourself away from your lady fair, we need to get back to work."

"He doesn't give a man a chance to appreciate the finer things," said Jed laughing. He placed a kiss on her cheek as he went by.

They entered the trees near the bluff. They were ready to start making the far sidewall of the corral and excited at the prospect.

As the afternoon wore on, the shade of the trees had moved to the side and the mare was in the sun. Beth got up to go move her and was hit by a strong feeling that everything was turning. She was nauseous, again, too. What is the matter with me, she thought? She held still for a moment and the feeling passed. The mare followed her to a cooler area with no trouble but as Beth tied the rope the feeling returned, stronger this time. She collapsed.

She was lying in the grass when Ben returned to get the water bag from the hut.

"Help, Jed!" he yelled. "It's Beth."

Jed ran to her. Ben sat on the grass with her head in his lap. He was fanning her face.

"Get the water bag, quick!" Jed raced for the water and returned with it.

"Did the mare kick her? Is she injured?"

"It doesn't seem like she is hurt," said Ben. They sprinkled a little water on her face and patted it and blew on her trying to cool her. She moaned, opening her eyes and tried to sit up.

"Lay still," ordered Jed. "What happened? Where did she kick you?"

Beth was still a little foggy, but she answered.

"She didn't kick me. I just got dizzy. That's all. I'm fine now." Once again she tried to get up, but Jed wouldn't let her. You stay right where you are. He ran in the hut and carried out bedding. He fixed a bed for her in the deepest shade and then picked her up like a baby and put her on the pallet tenderly.

"Beth, I couldn't stand it if anything ever happened to you. Please promise me that you will stay here and rest. Don't move. Don't do anything more but rest. Promise me!"

"Yes, I promise, but there is so much to do. I'm fine now, really," said Beth.

"No you aren't!" Jed was nearly shouting at her.

"You are exhausted. We should have seen it earlier. What was I thinking? Here is the water bag. Take a big drink. That's good, now I want you to stay here and take a nap. Promise me that you will."

"Yes, Yes, I promise, only stop getting so upset. I probably have been doing more than I should. Now you two, back to the fence! Don't use me as an excuse to slack off!" She tried hard to lighten the mood by kidding with them. "Have a drink and then back to work with you," she said.

The men wore looks of deep concern as they walked through the trees to the spot where they had been working.

"We have been letting her do too much. No more! I'm going to make sure that she rests. Even if she hates it, she is going to take a nap every day until she looks healthier," Jed declared.

Then they both tore into the project with a vengeance, as if working harder would make everything all right again. Every few minutes Jed crept back through the trees and peeked silently to check on Beth. He relaxed a little when he finally saw that she was curled up on her side, sound asleep.

"She is sleeping like a baby," Jed announced with a smile when he returned.

"Now we need to get a safe haven made for our other babies," said Ben, as he went back to work.

By sunset, the far fence wall was up, and the end wall was started and strongly fastened. They went to the river and washed the sweat off with a cool swim.

They had forgotten all about the mash and it had dried down to a scorched lump before the fire burned down to a soft glow. Ben took the pan to the river and scraped it out and scrubbed it with sand. He filled it half full of water and immediately put on a new batch of mash.

"That didn't help our supplies any. I should have pulled it off to the side when I was in there."

Jed carried Beth inside the hut. He didn't want her to expend any energy at all.

"You are treating me like a fragile princess," she said, "I could get used to this. Ugh! What is that awful smell?"

"That, Dear Princess, is the smell of burned mash. I forgot it," answered Ben.

Jed sat Beth near the fire and served her a large piece of roast. With that he gave her a handful of shelled out nuts rolled first in honey and then sugar.

"I want you to eat every bit of that," he said. He jumped up and got the coffee pot and a small pan. He started coffee brewing and then made a batch of his tonic. When she saw what he was doing, she objected.

"Oh, not that stuff again."

"Yes, that stuff every day until I see roses on fat cheeks! And that's an order."

"Yes sir," she joked. She did like the attention, but didn't like the look of concern she still saw on his face.

The subject changed then to the horses and the corral and where they would start the little water channel.

"I want to bring the little black foal in here by me tonight. Would you mind?" asked Beth. "She needs extra attention." The men thought that a horse inside the main room was not a good idea but they would not have denied her anything at that moment. They made a bed of hay, next to the wall and placed bedding for Beth and

Jed next to it. Ben thought it best not to try to take the foal in the bedroom. Ben put his bedding in there temporarily.

Stump came to the front door and they could hear him scratch to be let in.

"He has sure been gone a lot. I hope he isn't doing anything that he will regret," said Jed with a chuckle.

As Ben opened the door to let him in, he noted that the mare and foal had not been frightened by his arrival in the yard. He slipped out long enough to bring her and Ginger up close to the hut and gave them both some fresh water. He patted both of them and Angel seemed like she was quite comfortable having humans near, caring for her. I am sure that she was not wild, but a horse that the stallion had stolen from settlers somewhere. When he went back inside, he was smiling.

"That Angel is sure friendly. She acts like she has been with us a long time."

Jed poured coffee for Ben and put some in his own cup. He sat down on the mat near Beth. She was sipping her tonic as if it were poison.

"Ben I don't like to ask you, because you have already been doing so much, but would you check on the water and feed for the chickens? I did it this morning, but not since."

He told her he would do it right away before they started to move the horses and feed them. He said if he waited, it might get forgotten.

He pulled the mash away from the heat and went outside. He gave the chickens some grain, and fresh water, and smiled when he found another egg. This will make Beth smile, he thought. When he went inside, he handed her the egg. She laughed and then asked him to put it in the bowl in the back corner where she had the others, with a basket over them to insulate and hold the cool, from the rock wall.

He went in near the horses and moved slowly around touching them and talking to them. He put his arm around the little black one and led her in to the bed they had made for her. He tied her to the wall and suggested that Beth sit on her own bed to feed the foal.

Beth got up slowly. Afraid that the dizziness would return, she moved first to the center clothes tree, then around it to her bed. Both men noted her careful movements but didn't comment.

Ben got a small pan of the cooled mash. He stirred a little more water in it and brought it to her. Then he put a second pan nearby with some water in it.

"This is to rinse your hands off," he said. The foal found comfort and security in Beth's gentle touch and was soon eating. When she had finished, Beth rinsed off her hands in the water and asked for something, to use to wash the foal's face. She had mash all over it. By the time her face was clean, the foal had relaxed enough to lie down beside Beth in the dry grass. Beth wrapped her arm around the foal's neck and soon they were both asleep.

Jed and Ben mixed up the rest of the mash with water and quietly fed the rest of the foals. Buddy bunted Ben in the back and acted like he wanted to play. Ben scratched his ears and gave him a handful of dry grain.

"I don't think we need to give him much mash. He has been eating the hay all day."

The brown twins stood close together and it took a while to get them to eat.

"They still aren't sure what all this is about," said Jed.

"They will all like it better, when they can be outside in the corral," said Ben. "Now that they are fed, let's get these guys out in the triangle and clean this place out, so we can bring Angel and Ginger in," said Ben. The section of fence that they had left loose was just wide enough for the foals to walk through. They removed the ropes from their necks, and fastened the fence and made sure that every inch of the enclosure, sides and top were safe and secure.

They returned to rake out Ginger's area and put down fresh hay.

"As soon as the corral is done we will have to spend time cutting grass and finding grain. The grass won't be hard, but it will be a problem finding grain that is ready to use," said Jed. They filled the water baskets with fresh water and slid one of them into the triangle. Ginger and Angel went into the clean stall easily. Surprise stayed close to his mother and as soon as they were inside, he decided it was time to go to sleep. He lay in the grass against the wall and she soon joined him.

Ben was just closing the big door when he looked up to see the stallion on the other side of the river, just coming out of the trees.

"We brought the horses in, just in time. Look across the river." Jed looked and saw the stallion enter the water. His herd was with him. They latched the big door and made sure it was secure, and then they did the same to the front. Ben stepped into the bedroom, and opened the shutters. They wanted to be able to hear what was going on outside and to see the foals in the little triangle. All three foals were standing up looking in the direction of the river.

"Maybe we shouldn't have left them out there!" The alarm in Ben's voice added to Jed's tension.

"They will be fine," Jed assured him with more conviction than he felt. Ben propped his rifle against the wall by the window.

"I don't want to hurt him, but I would shoot him before I would let him take any of our horses."

Beth slept on. She was totally unaware of the drama going on around her.

"She is sleeping so soundly. Is she all right?" asked Ben.

"Yes, I am hoping that she will sleep right through all this. I gave her a mild sedative in that tonic. I thought that he might show up here just before total dark, and she has had enough stress to last her a life time."

"You are right about that," agreed Ben.

Just then they heard a big bang against the door to Ginger's area. He is after the mare! The horses were all standing now, even the little black foal. The heels of the stallion slammed into the door again. Ginger crowded against the door to the main room and whinnied. She was frightened and so was Angel.

Jed unlatched the door to the stall and went in with the horses, closing it behind him. He stood between them, with an arm around each of their necks. Another huge bang rocked that side of the stall.

"If he keeps that up he can knock the whole place down," said Ben. "He sure is determined to get in to them." A small trickle of dirt came from the ceiling above the fire pit. "See what I mean," shouted Ben sounding frantic. He grabbed a long, branch from the pile of firewood and lit it. Running into the bedroom with it, he thrust it out the window, holding the fire out in front of him. He climbed up onto the roof of the hut yelling and waving the burning branch at the stallion. The horse was so startled by this unusual sight that he turned in fear toward the river.

Ben jumped down and followed him with the fire, yelling and making strange growling sounds until the stallion entered the water and crossed to his waiting herd on the other side. Ben dropped the branch on top of the big rock and quickly made a pile of dry wood in the gravel halfway down the bank. He added his torch to the pile and soon the entire area was flooded in light. The stallion and his herd milled around on the other bank for a few moments then moved off into the trees and darkness of the night.

Jed opened the front door when it became quiet. He walked out into the tense atmosphere surrounding the hut. Jed carried his rifle, ready, in his hands.

"You idiot!" he shouted. "You could have been killed! Why would you do such a foolish thing? What if he had turned on you? His hooves can kill! Don't you know that he will probably double back and try again anyway? Let's get inside."

As they came back in the front door, Beth opened her eyes.

"What are you doing?"

"Just checking the horses and making sure everything is fine. Go back to sleep Honey," Jed answered, trying to keep the tension out of his voice. She coaxed the little horse back down and cuddled closer and went right back to sleep.

"I'm glad she slept through his visit," said Ben.

"Me, too, and I am sorry, Ben, for yelling at you," Jed said. He reached for the Bible and asked Ben to read something out loud for them for a while.

They added water to the coffee and sipped it while the words calmed their minds and bodies and awareness of the trust in His protection once again renewed their spirits. They went to bed soon after and slept for the few remaining hours of the night. The stallion didn't return to disturb them.

Jed was up first and started the mash cooking. He also started a new batch of tonic and some tea. After using the bluff to check the area, he put the ropes on Ginger and Angel and took them outside. When he saw the damage to the outside of her door, he was amazed that it held. He breathed a prayer of thanksgiving as he chose a new spot of grass for them to enjoy. He brought out a water basket and put it where they could both reach it. He cleaned up the stall and refreshed it, leaving the big door open until the foals were put in. "Today we will finish the corral for you ladies," he promised, giving each a loving pat as he went by. Ben came out the front door and looked bleary eyed at Jed.

"That was some night we had. I sure hope we don't have to do that often. How are the horses?" asked Ben.

"Everybody is fine." Beth is still asleep with her arms wrapped around that foal like it is a child. That horse is going to be so spoiled that it will think it is a princess."

"That might be the perfect name for that little lady. We will see if Beth thinks so when she wakes up," said Jed.

"If Beth thinks so, about what?" she asked, poking her head out the front door.

"Good morning Honey, and how do you feel?" asked Jed. "I think it is too soon to know. I feel like I am still asleep, yet I feel like I have been asleep for a week!" Just then the black foal wandered out the front door she had left open. "Oh, I am sorry. I forgot all about you being loose, little girl. I don't want you to wander off. I untied her from the wall last night. She was sucking my fingers. I think she has decided that I am her substitute mother," said Beth, as she put her arm around the foal's neck.

Jed explained about their conversation and asked if she liked the name "Princess." Beth was delighted and kept saying the new name as she led her back inside to feed her.

"We better feed the rest and get them back in the stall before she lets them all loose," said Jed, kidding. "Do you want to leave Buddy in the triangle today?"

"Yes," said Ben, "He will probably be happier outside. I'll go dump some grass in there and check his water. Let's move the twins inside though, with Princess."

They worked as a team and all the horses, chickens and Stump received a generous meal and attention. Breakfast was coffee for the men with a chunk of left over roast and for Beth, tonic, with a bowl of the mash with nuts in it and honey on top. "You need to eat every bit of it," Jed instructed.

He lowered the deer and felt bad that the meat had been neglected. It was starting to spoil. The hide was still good. He carried the carcass down to the area of the wolf den and dropped it under the trees, bringing back the hide. Ben staked it out next to the wolf pelt and buffalo hide and started scraping it. He tossed a scraper to Jed, who immediately knelt and worked the wolf skin.

Jed stuck his head in the door of the hut long enough to tell Beth to do nothing harder than petting the foals and the two men returned to the project of the corral fence.

They put six double strips of leather on the gate for hinges, and were joyous, when in early afternoon they were able to tell Beth that she could come and look at the corral. She was pleased and proud of them and said so.

"This is wonderful. You have both worked so hard, and now we have a safe place to put our new babies." She tried the gate and was able to swing and secure it back in place with no problem. She pushed on the fence and found that she couldn't budge it.

"I know that I am not very strong, but I can't make a creak or wobble in it," she said.

"We are going to stop for a bit and then dig the trench, but first I think we can put the foals out under the trees and let them have a little sunshine," said Jed.

"We better leave Buddy where he is until we put another foot or more of height on it, but the others can go in."

The twins and Princess trotted around happily until Beth walked away, and then Princess ran to the fence whinnying for her to come back.

"See that? She thinks she owns me," said Beth laughing. "Let's put the mares in there, too, so they don't have to be tied. They will be happier," said Beth.

They carried in water and then sat down in the grass to enjoy looking at their horses, in the corral.

"You need to be thinking of names for the twins, Ben. They will bond to you better if you start calling them by a name and it would probably be better if you are the one doing their feedings."

"Are you sure that you want me to claim both? After all, this whole thing was your idea and you have worked hard, too. I really want Buddy, but you can claim one of the browns or both and I won't be upset. It goes without saying that Angel and Surprise are yours and Princess has adopted Beth."

"Ben, if it weren't for you and the hut and Ginger and everything else, I wouldn't even have Beth! Don't argue. Just come up with some nice names."

"Let me see, the boy can be Rusty, and the girl can be Missy. Will those do?" asked Ben

"Those names are fine and in a way they seem to fit them," said Jed.

The men set to work marking the channel where the water would flow to the low spot. Ben started digging and Jed began collecting flat rocks to line the inside of it. They dug from the hollow out toward the river at a direction heading up stream. Instead of going in and out of the gate with the rocks, Jed dumped them rather unceremoniously over the fence, making sure the foals were clear of the immediate area.

Both of them were too busy to keep an eye on Beth. She had felt bad when the deer meat had spoiled. She felt she had failed to process it for drying. She was determined to make a good evening meal for her hard working, men. She stirred up the promised cake and greased Jed's heavy cast iron kettle. She clamped the lid on it and set it just off the coals. She chopped nuts and ground sugar to make it finer. She got out the precious buffalo fat and a pinch of salt, and stirred them together. She looked through the tins of spices that Ben had and added a sprinkle of cinnamon. The glaze was ready.

She set it aside and got Jed's fishing pole and went to the riverbank by the willow trees. It didn't take much to dig up a few worms and soon she was catching supper. Stump appeared in the trees behind her, but hesitated to come near. When Beth coaxed him, she realized that he wasn't alone. Standing behind him was a small gray wolf. She held perfectly still. She wasn't sure what she should do. She had broken Jed's first rule.

"Always take your gun with you if someone is not with you." He had made her promise. She feared that he would be furious. She could hear him saying it, in her head. "Always carry your rifle and be sure it is loaded!"

"God, please tell me what to do."

The wolf stayed back in the shade, but Stump came forward finally in his usual carefree manor.

"Stump, what have you done? Don't you know that wolves kill horses? Specially baby ones? Oh, Stump," Beth said, "Is she your lady? Is that where you go so much? You go to see her, don't you?"

Just then there was a tug on the line and Beth landed a foot long fish. As soon as it was on the grass, the wolf took a few steps forward. Beth soon figured out that the canines had come for a fish dinner. She handed the fish to Stump. He whirled and headed past the wolf into the trees and she followed close behind.

"Well what am I supposed to think of that?" she said out loud. She put a new worm on her hook and started to fish again.

She wasn't sure how long it had been so she jumped up and went to check her cake. It was done and perfectly golden brown. "That's a miracle," she said to the foals that were watching her intently through the fence. I was afraid that it was going to be burned. On impulse, she reached into the bag of sugar, putting a big pinch in her palm. She put a sprinkle on the lips of each one as she gave it scratches and talked to it. They licked and nudged for more. "No that's all for this time," she said as she returned to her fish line to find the worm gone and the pole nearly in the water. That must have been a large fish, she thought, or... a turtle? That thing looks like a floating rock, she thought. She watched him for a few minutes as he held his head above water, with his shell just beneath the surface. "If I could, I would catch you," she said to the surface of the water.

She tried another worm and promised herself that this time she would catch a fish and keep it. She did just that and two more. She cleaned them right there and let the turtle have what she didn't want as a bonus. She took her catch inside and put them in the frying pan with some grease. I won't put them near the fire yet, but I better start some more mash. She got the big pan and put water and grain in it and placed it where it would start to cook. I think after I feed the chickens, I'll go check on the progress of our water channel.

Buddy blew a greeting to her as she went past the triangle so she stopped to talk to him. He backed up and scuffed a front foot as she drew near.

"You are a big bluff, Buddy. I think you are more afraid than any of the others. You are a beautiful boy and you will be out of that little pen as soon as they can manage it." He came closer, sticking his muzzle out of a hole in the fence, and snorted at her. She tried to reach in to scratch him but he backed up each time.

"See what I mean. You are just a big baby."

She left him and went to see if the chickens had given her any eggs. As she walked through the trees she felt that she was being watched. It made her uneasy. She looked around, but didn't see anything unusual. The chickens were fine. She gave them some grain and fresh water, but found no eggs. "Taking the day off?" she asked as she left the little pen and latched the fence back in place.

Stump came over and sat beside her. She gave him a hug and scratches and then decided to find Ben and Jed. As she walked toward the corral, she had that feeling again that she was being watched. She automatically stroked Ginger, Angel and Surprise as she entered the gate and they turned their heads and watched her walk away. Their peaceful behavior soothed her uneasy feeling.

When she got nearer the front of the fence and called out to find Jed, he was already walking toward her, just inside the fence, followed by Ben.

"We have it dug as far as the front corner of the corral, but we need to gather more rocks for lining it. We are only half way with that," said Jed. They came out of the gate and chatted a bit, and then went to gather more of the flat rocks they still needed.

"Beth, you have been working. I can tell," Jed said sternly. "Your cheeks are hot. You look tired. Please go in and take a nap."

"I have not done anything hard," She objected. "Do you call fishing hard work?" "Did you catch any?" "Four, no five" but I gave one to Stump and his friend and a turtle took one."

"A turtle, I would like to catch him," said Ben. "They are good to eat."

"Did you say that you gave a fish to Stump and a friend? What friend." asked Jed? "He has a wolf that he had with him. I'm sure that it was pretty young, it was smaller than he is."

"Bold One," Jed and Ben said, at the same time, and laughed. "The wolf den must be full again, if she is back," said Ben. "I don't like the idea of a pack of wolves so close to our horses," said Jed. "The little ones are so vulnerable. Even in the corral the wolves can get them. They can climb right over the fence or dig under."

"I thought you said the wolves were friendly." Concern filled Beth's voice with a tight sound.

"I don't think they would hurt any of us, but they are wild animals. Wild wolves eat horses!" said Jed.

"What are we supposed to do?" she asked. I don't want you to kill the wolves, but I don't want to have one of our babies killed, either."

"For now, they are safe because we are working out here near them. We will have to build a barn big enough to hold all of them," said Ben.

"I don't want to even think about any of this," she said. "I am going in and stir the mash and make a pot of tea." She put the coffee pot on with a big batch of tea in it, made with chamomile, lemon grass and mint. That will go well with the fish, she thought. The mash was done. She pulled it to the side and added some more water, giving it a quick stir.

She pulled down one of the large gathering baskets hooked on the ceiling in the bedroom. She had made several. This time she remembered to take her rifle. She made sure it was loaded and left for the trail to the garden. After a few steps, she turned around and went back in and filled her pockets with bear jerky. I don't really care for the taste of that, she thought. I don't know why I am bothering to take jerky for wolves when we will probably have to shoot them to keep them from hurting the horses. She thought about the situation all the way to the garden.

Once in the garden the beautiful rows of growing vegetables soothed her and she forgot all about the wolves while she filled her basket with two small red tomatoes, a few half grown carrots, and their biggest head of cabbage. She looked at the corn, beets and peas. They weren't ready yet. The pepper plants had their purple and white blossoms now. The corn was almost up to her shoulders. That is growing fast, she thought. The sunflowers were keeping up with the corn. She wondered how high they would get. The little marigolds were making yellow and orange splashes between the tomato plants. She picked a couple small blossoms. They are so cheerful, she thought.

She glanced over at the little lake and the hill beyond. The ducks paddled near the edge, making circles in the water. It seemed that something in that direction had changed, but she couldn't be sure. She shook her head and decided she was wrong. She latched the gate and headed up the trail to the hut. Her mind was on the delicious meal they would have. She shuddered when she crossed the spot where the black wolf had nearly attacked her. I will never forget the look of his face snarling at me, she thought. She stopped and peered under the pine branches. She couldn't see the den from where she stood but she was afraid to go any closer.

"Oh no," she said out loud. "I left my gun leaning against the fence by the garden gate." I don't like carrying that thing; it's so heavy, she thought.

When she turned around to go get it, three nearly grown wolves and Stump blocked her path. All of them were about ten feet away. Stump's tail was wagging, but the younger ones moved their tails very little, seeming nervous. She couldn't help but smile.

"You are just a bunch of treat lovers," she said, as she handed Stump a piece of jerky. Deciding to try to give one to Bold One, too, she lowered herself so she would seem less frightening. She extended the jerky as far as she could. Her arm grew tired, but she held it there. The female stared at her face and came forward so slowly that Beth could barely see her move.

Finally Bold One reached for the jerky and took it so gently that Beth could not be sure when she actually transferred the meat to the wolf's mouth. Bold One quickly backed up a few feet and started to chew it. Beth put two more pieces on the ground and tossed a third on the ground closer to the den thinking the mother was probably in there. Standing up slowly and moving toward the garden she looked behind her. Stump was following and behind him just a few feet was Bold One.

A search of her pockets provided one last piece. She wanted to try to feed her again. With it divided, she got down on her knees and extended a piece in each hand. Stump quickly took the one extended toward him, and once again the wolf locked eyes with Beth as she came forward. She took the jerky and ate it in one gulp. Beth wished she could touch her.

Standing up, she dusted her knees, and then got her gun and hurried back toward the hut.

"They are just big dogs that have never been loved," she told herself. "No, they aren't! They kill to eat. Dogs don't do that. But that's because no one feeds them. If they were loved and fed they wouldn't have to kill other animals." She argued with herself audibly, as she walked along carrying the rifle and basket of garden produce.

When she was nearly all the way back to the hut, she rounded the curve in the trail. She met Jed who was looking for her.

"Honey, I thought you were taking a nap! What are you doing out here alone? You could be killed! I worry about you."

"What would hurt me, the turtle?" She tried to be light about it but he was tired and concerned and a little cranky.

"I took my rifle and checked it. It is loaded, just the way you said. Please Jed, don't be angry. I just wanted to get some vegetables to make a nice meal for you. You both have been working so hard." She wasn't used to anyone caring so much about her that they worried. She had grown up as rather a free spirit. Her father encouraged her independence and her mother was just so busy with other things that she seldom inquired into the activities of Elizabeth's day. Riding lessons, piano lessons, and French lessons along with her tutor all had been arranged to keep her busy and out of the way.

CHAPTER TEN   THE STALLION'S LOOKOUT

They walked toward the hut and movement took their eyes to the top of the bluff. The stallion stood there glowering down on them. The evening sun shone on his coat and the wind blew his tail and mane giving him the look of movement, even though he was standing still.

"He must have found a path up there from the other side.

"Let's start moving the horses in quickly." When they looked up again he had disappeared. They put all the horses inside this time, even Buddy. He was glad to be out of isolation, but not happy to be put in with the others. He wanted to stretch his legs and run.

"Tomorrow Buddy, I promise, that I will take you out with Ginger for a run," said Ben.

Jed had calmed down about Beth not napping and apologized to her for being cross. They all worked quickly to get all the horses in and comfortable. The big door was closed and latched. Buddy presented his face over the half door and curled his lips in a way that looked like he was either smiling or getting ready to sneeze. It made Beth laugh. She pulled the tops off the baby carrots and handed them to Ben.

"Here is a treat for your funny Buddy. You can try these outer cabbage leaves on Angel and Ginger. I don't know if horses eat cabbage, but I'm sure that rabbits do. It is a good thing that you made the bottom of the fence close together or we would have rabbits eating everything in the garden. It all looks so delicious."

She chopped up the cabbage and put it on to cook, sliced the tomatoes and then set the pan of fish on to fry. Ben slipped out the front door after a few minutes, unnoticed. He prepared the fire pit outside that he used to dry meat. He thought he might need to keep it burning later. He whistled and was glad when Stump came running out of the trees. They came in together. He liked it best when his family was together and safe. My family, Ben thought. It sure has grown.

It was a good thing that most of the horses were small yet. They were crowded. Missy was the next to stick her head over the door. Beth reached over and gave her a good scratch.

"Missy, you would be in here with Princess if I let you, wouldn't you?" Beth stuck her finger in the sugar tin and let Missy lick it.

None of the foals seemed to be afraid of the fire. Jed wondered why until he saw Beth giving them sugar.

"No wonder they aren't afraid to stick their heads out here, you are providing them with sweets," he kidded her and wrapped his arms around her.

"They aren't the only ones having treats. Wait until you see what we have for desert." She uncovered the cake, and poured the glaze on it. "When did you have time to bake that?"

"I stirred it up this afternoon."

"It looks delicious, but what is that awful smell?"

"That is the cooked cabbage, and it is good for you."

"Let's put it outside and it will keep that stallion away," said Jed.

"Jed you stop that. You have to eat some of it!"

"Honey I am just teasing. I will enjoy it. I like cabbage, but you must admit it smells terrible."

"Where did you go, Ben?" Beth asked as he came in the front door. "I was just preparing wood in the fire pit outside. I think I will light it soon. Maybe it will help discourage the stallion from coming close,"

"You really think he will come, don't you?" Jed deliberately didn't answer her question.

"When can we eat? I am starving."

"We can eat right now. Everything is ready." "It all smells wonderful, Beth." said Ben. "I love cabbage, cooked or raw."

Before they ate they held hands and prayed a prayer of thanksgiving for the day they had, and silently Beth included thanks that she had fed the wolves and was making friends of them. They prayed for protection for all of them through the night and then asked a blessing on their food.

The stallion had climbed back up to the spot high on the bluff. He was watching the Indians slowly ride by on the outside of the trees, on the other side of the river. This was the third time he had observed them pass this way. He hated and feared people. Suddenly he made a decision. He whirled and hurried down the path to his waiting herd, where he stomped and displayed his displeasure at having to leave his mare and the foals behind. The Stallion headed away at a steady pace. He wanted to put distance between his herd and the offending humans. The Indians had no idea of the good they had served by being there at just that moment. Their presence had turned the tide in the battle to keep the horses.

*****

The leader of the Winahatah warriors, Growling Bear, sniffed the air again as his eyes searched the ground for any sign that the covered wagon had been there. Had he walked around to the back of the big oak tree near the river, he would have seen the mound of stones between the roots and the cross with the names and date that Ben had carved on the trunk.

"I know that it stopped here by this huge oak. There are evil spirits at work. I can smell it in the air. Can you smell it?" The others nodded, puzzled by the unfamiliar odor of the cooking cabbage.

"We must leave here and return to our village." He turned his back to the river and headed the search party home, back to their village. He dreaded admitting to Chief Dark Wolf, that he had failed. They had not found the broken wagon or the book with the words of the powerful God that Brave Sparrow worshiped.

"Why do they want to learn about a God that a small white girl talks about? She should be punished and taught to honor our spirits only." His thoughts were like heavy gray clouds around him. The others in his scouting party did not speak. They knew him well and knew that it was best not to try to talk to him when he was angry.

*****

The night was quiet. Beth listened to an owl in the distance. Jed slept soundly after his day of hard work. His arm stretched across her waist. If someone had asked her, she would not have been able to express all her feelings at that moment, but she knew that she was happier than she had ever been in her life.

When she married James, it was different. She knew that she loved him but marrying him had been a way to get away from her parents and their world. He was reckless and sometimes she felt insecure with him. She had married him to escape her life in the big impressive house, filled only by fancy furniture and pompous strangers. Her parents loved her but not enough to really ever hear what she tried to say. God did.

Even when she felt she had made a terrible mistake taking the wagon train, God had surely protected her and directed her here to Jed's arms and a life that was perfect. She listened to the sound of the leaves moving in the breeze as it came over the bluff and crossed the river. The song of a night bird lulled her to sleep.

Ben got up early. In the morning sunshine, he tied a rope to a soft bridle on Buddy and fastened it to a loop on his saddle.

"Let's go play out in the grass for a while," he said. He had fashioned a loop of light leather around Ginger's jaws with a rope on either side of her head for reins. He had been on her back as they walked along, but he had never really ridden her. Today he was going to let her run with Buddy and then he planned to try to ride and direct her. He tied the reins up on her back so they wouldn't get tangled and turned the two horses loose on the prairie. He knew that he was taking a chance. He had done his best to check the area from the top of the bluff, for the stallion and his herd, but if she wanted to go to him, she could still head out and he had no way of stopping her.

The crisp morning air was invigorating to the two young horses. As soon as they were released on the prairie, they headed away from Ben at a swift gallop. Buddy had no trouble keeping up with Ginger. He was smart enough to follow and not fight the lead fastened to the saddle.

They were a beautiful pair. Ben watched as their speed decreased and Ginger started to circle around. Buddy bucked a bit, as if he objected. He must think he is going back in that little triangle right away, thought Ben. Ginger brought him up to Ben and stopped. They were not breathing hard or tired yet. Ben reached up and untied the reins. He scratched ears and patted both horses talking to them. As he slid up onto Ginger's back, she didn't show any sign of displeasure. Ben was not a heavy man. His weight was far less than she could carry. She just considered his weight on her back as an extended hug. She loved him and liked it when he was close.

He leaned forward and held her neck and softly whispered.

"OK Ginger, let's go." She started to walk at the usual slow pace. He sat up straight and looked back at Buddy. He was walking along beside her as if this was a lot of fun. Ben wasn't sure what he had done but her speed increased. Buddy had to run to keep up. Ben hung on tight and pulled back on the reins a little, she slowed down a bit.

"Good girl," he praised her. They practiced turning, gently to the right in a big circle and then to the left. He continued to watch Buddy for any sign of tiring. He was still frisking around and enjoying the whole thing when Ben called an end to the lesson for the day.

It had gone really well and he didn't want to do anything to ruin it. He had actually ridden Ginger and she had followed his direction. He wasn't sure what he had done to speed her up, but he would develop signals with her as time went on.

He put her in the corral with Buddy. He lengthened Buddy's rope and fastened him to a tree that stood inside away from the fence, and the gate.

"I don't want you sailing over the fence before we get it made taller," he said, as he tied the rope. He brought in some water for them and then went back in to check the pan of mash he had started. He heard a cackle from the chicken pen and smiled at the thought of another fresh egg. We better try to always keep a few back so that if one of the hens wants to hatch them, we will have a few to put under her. I will mention it to Beth when she gets up, he thought.

No one mentioned the stallion, but they had not forgotten him. They were all happy that he had not come again. They had fallen into a morning routine of chores. Soon all the animals had been fed and watered. Beth worked at getting their areas cleaned so the men could work on the corral and channel. She retrieved two eggs from the chicken pen and that's when Ben remembered to suggest that she always rotate the eggs and keep a few on hand that were fresh in case one of the hens decided they wanted to sit and hatch some.

Ben entered the gate to the corral with Princess and Jed brought the twins on leads. They were followed by Beth bringing Angel and Surprise. She talked to Buddy and scratched his neck and he loved every moment of attention.

"It is good that he can be in here and you can keep an eye on him while you finish our water channel."

By noon they had all but the last foot dug and lined with rocks. When they pulled that last foot of sand and gravel out of the way, the water started to flow through the channel as they had planned. They had a piece of slate and a large rock ready to use when they thought they had enough water in the pond, all they had to do was put them in the mouth of the channel to stop the flow.

Even before they entered the corral to see how deep the water had become, they saw Rusty standing in the middle of the little pond stomping and having fun. They laughed at his antics.

"We will have to keep track of it to see how long the water takes to soak in, but after a few times the ground should become saturated and the water will stay longer. Let's work on making the fence higher and then we can plan the barn.

By nightfall, the fence had been extended to above Jed's head, all the way around. In many places the fence met the growing branches of the trees. They worked well as a team. The water hole stayed full after the fourth filling. The ground was becoming soft in and around it. They talked about dragging in gravel from the riverbed to stabilize it.

After a quick swim, the men walked up to the hut. Three rabbit furs were scraped and drying on the grass. The front door of the hut stood open and rabbits roasted above the fire, but Beth was not in sight. She came down the path from the woods up river.

"Where did you go?" asked Jed. Ben noticed her basket full of greens and a few stems of wild grapes.

"I have supper ready. The corral looks great. I noticed it earlier when I went down to the garden to get some tomatoes, oh, and the wolves are gone again." Jed took the heavy basket from her, noticing how tired she looked. I went exploring and I found a wild grape vine. We can dry some when they are riper. Maybe I could make jam. We can ask Sam if he has jars when we go back to the settlement to trade.

"Good idea," said Jed.

Ben asked if they had seen Stump and no one had since morning. His frown showed his concern.

"He will be fine. He is probably with Bold One," said Beth.

"You are right. I just worry that he might not come back one day. He takes on any animal he feels is threatening. He doesn't seem to know any limitations to his ability. He would try to protect her, no matter what."

They enjoyed their meal and the conversation soon turned to the barn and where it should be and how it was to be built. Stump walked in and greeted everyone but seemed restless. He went back out and then came in again.

"Something is bothering Stump," said Ben. "Guess I'll go look around." He picked up his rifle and went out the side door. After a few minutes he came back in.

"I don't see anything but we need to get the horses in for the night, anyway." They all went to the corral and helped transfer them. After feeding them all and getting them settled, they sat outside for a while and enjoyed the summer evening.

"The corn is going to be ready to eat soon, and I think I can start drying some of the tomatoes. The vines are loaded with green ones," said Beth. "The pepper plants seem to be a little behind. Next year, we should put them closer to the middle so they get more sun. Do you think that would help them?" asked Ben.

"It might or maybe we should try starting them inside and put out little plants instead of seeds," said Jed.

"I think we haven't enough light inside to get them to grow," said Beth. "The peas are ready to pick, too, but we need to leave some on the vine for seeds, the same with the string beans. We really have a bounty of vegetables. We will be eating well this winter."

"Maybe we can save lots of seeds and take them to the trading post. I think that lots of folks would like to have them," said Beth. "Beth, did I tell you that the row of corn by the pumpkins is popcorn? We will sure have fun with that this winter."

"No, I don't remember you telling me that. I would have picked it and boiled it to eat like the rest. It is a good thing you told me now."

"God is so good," said Ben. "It will be fun to pop our own, home grown corn at Christmas and string it on our tree." "Hey you have got to get the summer over before you start planning winter," laughed Jed.

I vote for making the barn out of logs and it can be a sod roof." "Where would be the best place to build it? I would like it to open into the corral and not too far from the hut. There is a clearing by the far back corner of the corral that would work," said Ben, "but is that too far to walk in really bad weather?"

"That's where I was thinking," said Jed. "The snow gets deep and piles up against the bluff where there aren't as many trees, but that won't be a problem if we make the door on this side facing the hut." "OK let's do it as soon as possible. I would like to start cutting and dragging logs tomorrow morning," said Jed. "It should go pretty smoothly with Ginger to move them," offered Beth.

"That dear girl has sure been a helper," said Ben with a warm smile.

"You know, don't you, that with that coloring she is probably related to the stallion, too. She almost matches him. She is just a little darker," said Beth. Ben was amazed that he hadn't thought of that until Beth said it.

"I'm glad she doesn't have his bad temper!" He said. They all laughed at that, remembering the scene at the circle when the stallion had attacked and tried to smash the gate, to free his mares.

The next day was Sunday and when the three of them remembered, they decided to relax, take a picnic and gathering baskets and see what they could find in the woods on the far side of the lake. Jed filled his two big baskets with herbs for cooking and healing. Ben spotted more grape vines covered with little green grapes. He pulled one off and put it in his mouth.

"Oh! That is so sour. They are definitely not ripe." He filled both his baskets with small green apples. Beth gathered cattail roots, and a bundle of their leaves for weaving. They found a spot where the grass was soft and the wild flowers scented the air with their perfume. Ben opened his Bible to Psalm 23 NIV and read out loud as they all relaxed and enjoyed the shade and the beautiful day.

"The Lord is my shepherd; I lack nothing. He makes me lie down in green pastures; He leads me beside quiet waters. He refreshes my soul: He guides me along the right paths for his name's sake. Even though I walk through the darkest valley, I will fear no evil, for you are with me. Your rod and your staff, they comfort me. You prepare a table before me in the presence of my enemies. You anoint my head with oil; my cup overflows. Surely your goodness and love will follow me all the days of my life; and I will dwell in the house of the Lord forever." NIV

"I love that Psalm. Every one of us can say that it has been proven true in our own experiences. God's hand was surely there protecting us all the way in the face of the enemy," said Jed.

"The earth is the Lord's and everything in it; the entire world, and those that live in it," said Beth. "All that we have we owe to Him."

"Amen." said Ben.

"We have come a long way just since I got here this summer. God has taken care of us and the horses are beautiful and our garden holds such a wonderful abundance. He is just so good," said Beth.

"I think that God has led the stallion and his herd away. We have been looking and haven't seen any sign of him for several weeks. That's certainly a blessing," said Jed.

The next weeks, the two men took food and water to the woods early each day and cut trees to use for the barn. They had cut and brought back enough logs for the walls. The next weeks, were still focused on the barn, but between chores and time out for the Bible on Sunday, the walls were slow going up even with the help of the clever contraption they had made to slide the logs up in place. Ginger and Angel struggled to pull the logs up the ramp and hold them steady until they were pegged into place. The opening for the big doorway wasn't framed in until the end of the sixth week. The following two weeks saw the roof go on.

A gentle rain had softened the prairie and made cutting the blocks of sod, an easier job. Ginger and Angel pulled the blocks back to the new barn on a big skid. The beams were layered with bundled willow twigs from around the lake, also grass was thatching on top of that. The sod went on top of a waterproof roof that was strong and secure. They made several shuttered window openings for light and air to circulate. The doors were fashioned like the front door of the hut but wider and the two doors closed to the middle with a big wooden bar.

They built seven stalls. That left a large open area, which could later be divided, if they needed it.

"This barn is a marvel! You built it big and strong and bright," enthused Beth as she helped pack the mud and grass mortar between the logs of the walls.

"We will make a loft up above the stalls for the hay. All that wood in the corner is cut to the right length and ready for building it," said Ben. "This big bin on the side is for the grain. The open area in the back is for the plow and any other tools that we have," explained Jed.

"It looks like you thought of everything," she replied.

"Tomorrow we will bring the horses in for the first time. We want to cut fresh hay for the stalls and braid ropes for some of the stalls yet. We can do that tonight. We need to tie Buddy. I think Rusty, Missy and Princess will stay settled, once they learn where their stall is located," said Jed. "Ben wants to use the big one in back for Angel and Surprise. He says he just wants to put a branch across the opening for Angel and Ginger. You can see the slots he made to slide them in."

"It is all so wonderfully big, and airy and organized," said Beth.

"We still need to make an oven for you, before the fall rains come and help harvest and preserve the rest of the garden," said Ben.

"We have all been so busy. I hope that nothing is being wasted," said Beth.

"After we get the barn ready, we will have to all work on the garden and bring back whatever is ready to harvest."

That evening they sat near the fire and made the ropes for the stalls from strips of leather. From the long prairie grass they made cords, to string the vegetables up near the ceiling. They soon had a small version of an overhead clothesline passing back and forth, suspended over the fire pit of the hut. The next day they brought in their first real harvest.

They made very thin slices of the tomatoes and bell peppers to hang. The poppy seeds were gathered in their round gray pods and piled in a basket made of cattail reeds. Some of the sunflowers were bright yellow and still beautiful but those that had bloomed early in the season had seeds in spiraling rows in their center and were ready to be picked. Ben cut the heads from the stems and piled them on the old sheet. He was surprised when he lifted the load to carry it to the barn.

"These are heavy," he said. Beth pinched off the dried heads of the marigolds, separating the bright yellow from the orange and rust. She was amazed at the small baskets filled with seeds she had. The plants were still blooming so they would have even more. The bean pods were turning tan and soon would be dry enough to pick. Ben looked forward to the time they could sit together and pop out the white beans. Beth was thinking that they would be delicious in soups when the weather turned cold. They would strip the vines, dropping the dry pods into a big basket, but not yet.

Jed volunteered to take the sunflower heads to the barn and returned with the sheet and bundled some of the colorful vegetables for the cache in the bedroom. The popcorn was left to stand a bit longer. They wanted to be sure it would be ripe for popping. Beth removed the curtain from the bedroom doorway and after two large slabs of slate were coated with the wet seeds of tomatoes and peppers, she covered them with the curtain, to keep them from the birds while they dried in the sun. They had saved several stalks of the sweet corn and the ears were left to dry further. Squash filled one half of the largest cache and pumpkins formed a row down the back wall of the bedroom where it was coolest.

"We should be able to pick the wild grapes as soon as the first frost hits. That will make them sweet. I want to dry some for raisins and make jam with some, so I plan to pick plenty."

"I hope the birds don't get to them before we do. That's what happened to the raspberries," explained Ben. "The bushes are where we cross the river. I can show you next time we are down there."

Stump had been in and out often but always seemed well fed and preferred attention and scratches to food. His coat was getting thick again. The feel of fall was in the air in the mornings when they got up.

Once the oven bricks were made and dried in the sun, it was quite easy to build the oven. It was plastered inside and out with heavy clay and built over a small pit for the fire. Stones held a thin piece of slate suspended over the fire area to serve as a rack. The chimney stood against the bluff and the door was a thick slab of slate. They lit a small fire in it to harden the plaster and after a day of constant heat it was ready for use.

Ben was thinking that they could make wild cherry pie now, but Beth's wish was for a loaf of fresh bread and she planned to get a yeast ball from the ladies in the settlement when they went to trade.

Jed told Beth that he wanted to leave for the Trading Post, as soon as they could get all the things ready that they wanted to trade. He had a list of things that they wanted to bring back.

In the next two evenings, Jed made two strong ropes to trade. He had a stack of cups and bowls made that they didn't really need. Ben had carved two bone crosses, two angels and three knives, during the evenings. Beth had generously refilled the packets that Ben's mother had made for seeds and placed them back in the rusted tin box. These they would keep but for the rest of the seeds, she had made many more packs to take to trade.

While cutting wood for the barn, they had located some wild cherry trees that were very old. They had gathered baskets full of the sour cherries to pit and dry for pies and Ben had brought back several pieces of their wood and both Jed and Ben had made lovely containers with lids. They had carved flowers and birds on them.

They had belts of braided leather, utility baskets and decorated ones.

"Once the cradle is in the canoe, we can fit all the rest of this stuff in and around it," said Jed, as he dragged the boat out, checking to be sure that it was still in good condition. He checked the seams and applied pitch here and there where it was needed.

"Are you sure you don't want to walk and use Ginger to take all that stuff?" asked Ben. "You know that it has to be carried, along with the canoe around the rapids and water falls." "It will be fine. I have done it alone and Beth won't need to carry anything. The canoe is very light," said Jed, "and so are the things we have to trade. We won't have the cradle on the way back. Don't be such a worrier, Ben."

"I can't help it. I still can picture her the way she was when we found her."

"Ben, you know that I would never carelessly endanger Beth. We won't be gone any longer than we have to," said Jed. "I plan on staying there only one night, or maybe two if Beth wants to visit more with those babies, but really I want to get back home."

"That's good," said Ben. "I will not like having you both gone, although I have lots to do."

They collected everything for the journey, and packed, carefully. Jed planned to leave the next morning at daybreak. Ben knew he was being childish, but he didn't like being left behind. He had volunteered to stay to take care of the animals, but now that he had a family again, he didn't want to ever be alone.

CHAPTER ELEVEN   WE HAVE COME A LONG WAY

The breeze seemed to play at pushing the canoe along. They spent one night alongside the river. Jed made a cozy shell by tipping the canoe on its side. The next morning he cut branches and made a travois to take the canoe and its contents around the waterfall and rapids. By noon of the second day they pulled their canoe up on the bank of the Hickory a short distance from the Trading Post.

"Even though the water got a bit rough where the Silver spills into the Hickory, this was a good trip," said Beth.

"It's a good way to travel," grinned Jed. He was pleased that she had enjoyed his canoe.

They were amazed to see the changes that had been made over the summer. Another house stood nearby, and a small building with a cross on the door now served as a church on Sunday for the growing community. People poured out of buildings to greet them and soon Jed and Beth were in a circle of hugs and smiles. A couple of men helped Jed to carefully lift his canoe farther from the river. A big fire burned in front of the store. Helen looked up at the group coming toward her. She had been tending the cooking of a large deer. They hugged and talked. Sam came out of the house with Abe on one arm and Henry running behind him.

"Look at Abe, how he has grown! Henry is so handsome. He looks like you, Sam," said Beth, reaching out to take Abe. Just then Tom and Gentle Fawn joined the group. Each one carried one of the twins. Tom tossed Stormy into the air and the baby boy laughed out loud. Annie shyly tucked her head into Gentle Fawn's neck, hiding behind the screen of her mother's soft black hair. She wouldn't turn around to look at Beth or Jed. The women hugged, pressing Abe and Annie in between them. Rose came out to see what all the commotion was about. Jed took Abe so that Beth could go hug Rose. As soon as Jed's arms lifted him away from Beth, he let out a howl.

"OK, little man, I think it is time to give you back to your mother," Jed laughed as he carefully handed the boy to Helen. The roasting deer soon turned into a feast as other food was brought out to share and as stories were told between bites of the tender venison.

"Beth you look much better now. You have put on a little weight, and you have rosy cheeks and a shine on your hair. I am so glad to see you looking so healthy and pretty."

"Thank you Gentle Fawn, I have been well fed. They spoil me."

"I am the one that is well fed. Look at me, I'm getting fat!" said Jed, as he put his arm around Beth. "She is a great cook."

They talked long into the night, laughing and sharing events of the time they had been separated. Everyone was amazed at the story of how they trapped the horses.

Helen invited them to sleep at their house.

"It is finished now and we have plenty of room for you," she said.

In the morning they carried all the trade goods into the store and Tom put on his official, trading hat. First Jed gave him the carved cradle, and thanked Tom for trusting him.

"Anytime," was his reply. "Well, I will need a few things and if they cost more than my trade goods are worth, I hope you will trust me again until I make it back." Jed named the usual things, coffee, salt, sugar, flour, and then he picked out a scythe and a sickle. "These will make gathering the hay for the horses a lot easier," he said. He encouraged Beth to pick out some fabric and thread. She chose a dress length of pretty yellow calico and a bolt of plain white cotton. She knew that she could dye it with natural colors, when she decided on its use.

She left the store with Gentle Fawn to help prepare a lunch and as soon as they were gone, he handed Sam a soft yellow wool blanket, "She seems to prefer yellow," he said, "I'll take a piece of this red and white oil cloth about six feet long and a length of that soft white flannel, too. She will make something nice. She didn't say it but I know she will need thread and scissors and a pack of needles."

"I need a wood plane, a couple bags of nails, a hammer and two windows, big ones. "We will be starting our house as soon as we get back, but I won't need the windows until spring. I will come back alone to get them."

"Will you be able to take those upstream?" asked Sam.

"No probably not. I will have to borrow Ginger and go the long way. I was thinking that I might use some wagon wheels we have, to make some sort of a small wagon. Beth doesn't know about us working on the cabin, so if you could keep it a surprise, I would appreciate it. Ben and I have been cutting trees every chance we get and have quite a few down and cleaned up. We are hoping that somehow, she won't know until the cabin is built."

"Jed, that sounds like an impossible goal. Women always know what we are doing. Did you and Ben register your place with the land office yet? You don't want to get that place all fixed up nice and have someone else come along and claim it. That new building down at the end of the row with the cross on the door is where you need to go. On Sunday it serves as our church but during the week it is the land office."

"Thanks; I didn't know a thing about it. I'll go down there right now and talk to them."

When Jed came out of the registrar's office, he was very troubled. He hoped that Ben would understand why it was necessary to put Beth's name on the papers. He had claimed Ben's acres in Beth's name and another One hundred and sixty acres in his own. He folded the papers and tucked them deep inside his pocket. They spent two days visiting and on the following morning they found themselves heading home with gray skies overhead and a light drizzle coming down. Tom had used an old, well-oiled hide to cover the bundles in the canoe.

"That won't keep you dry, but maybe it will keep the rain off the stuff you bought." Sam said it with a big smile.

"Thanks Tom. We will probably see you next spring."

As Jed pulled hard at the paddle and fought his way clear of the turbulent current where the rivers joined, his face showed the stress of his thoughts. He expertly pulled against the river but he did it automatically.

He was thinking of Ben and his reaction, when he told him that he had claimed the land where the hut stood. Why do I have to tell him at all? I could keep still about it, and later change it to his name when he is old enough. He doesn't know any more than I did that this territory has been opened up for homesteading. He won't find out. Jed's thoughts kept his mind busy.

Beth sat in the back of the canoe trying to paddle and match his strokes but she wasn't strong enough to keep up the unrelenting pace he was setting. She called out to him.

"Jed, can we stop to rest soon? I'm getting pretty tired." They were both soaked to the skin, by the cold rain that fell steadily. When Jed signaled to paddle to the gravel bank ahead, she was relieved. He seemed driven, and she was troubled that he hadn't shared with her what was bothering him. He had paddled so intensely that they had made it back to the place where they would have to portage around the rapids and falls.

Beth was shivering as she stepped out of the canoe into the edge of the water and helped pull it up onto the bank. After they carried everything up to the trail that went along the route of the rapids and the falls, Jed efficiently created a roof with the canoe and started a small fire against the rocks. He used a set of fire sticks that he kept with him in his bundle and collected a few branches from the underside of dense pines. Dry wood was at a premium but they found enough to warm themselves while they ate the sandwiches that Helen had given them. Beth cuddled close to Jed and asked if everything was all right.

"Sure, Honey, what could be wrong? Sam loved the cradle and we got two lanterns for the seeds plus the lamp oil, and some extra wicks. We will make good use of the sickle and Sam gave me an old bridle that I can take the fittings off to make a new one for Ben to use with Ginger. I bought an extra set at the blacksmiths shop, too, so we can start to train Angel. I think she is ready. She was an excellent help with building the barn."

"I think it will be fun to ride her when she is trained. I used to ride horses at home," said Beth.

"Mother thought it wasn't lady like, but my father just told me to be careful and have a good time," said Beth.

"We had lots of horses, but they were not as sweet as Angel and Ginger. I think it all depends on how they are treated to start with. Ben is such a sweet, kind kid; he wouldn't know any other way to treat a horse or person for that matter," said Beth.

"Yes," agreed Jed, "He is someone I would trust with my life." Trust, that word, slammed into his thoughts. He knew he would be taking advantage of Ben's trust if he didn't tell him about the papers. He didn't want to think about it anymore.

"Beth, are you still happy here, living in a hut with dirt floors and cleaning up after horses and cooking on a camp fire?"

"Jed, how can you ask such a thing? I love my life and I love you. I would never want to go back east. What made you ask that?"

"I love you so much, Beth, I guess I needed to hear you say that you are happy."

"Yes, Jed, I am happier than I have ever been in my whole life. Now let's talk about our friends. What did Sam have to say about that beautiful cradle?"

"He wants me to bring him two more in the spring!" said Jed with a proud smile.

"Someday I want you to make one for us. Maybe we will have a whole passel of kids. Would you like that, Jed?"

"You know I would. I want big strong boys and beautiful girls that look like you." Beth placed her hand on her tummy under the blanket and smiled to herself. She wasn't ready to share what she suspected. She wanted to be sure. They cuddled there for a while longer and watched the tiny river of water running off the side of the canoe.

"Rose gave me a yeast ball and so did Gentle Fawn and I have three great recipes to try out on you."

"You sound like I am a taste tester."

"Well you are!" She said with a hearty laugh.

"Beth the rain is almost stopped. Let's load this stuff on the travois and get up and around the falls before it gets totally dark. With the grass and leaves all wet, that thing will pull like it is on ice."

"I'm fine now and the air seems a little warmer. I think the cloud cover is thinning. We should be able to travel for quite a while before dark." Jed pulled the branches and leaves off the travois where he had hidden it in the brush. His deer hide was soaked, but it was strong and once again he loaded the canoe on it with all of its contents.

As predicted, the travois pulled easily. The clouds never completely cleared as Jed had hoped. Instead it grew dark earlier than usual and when they got to the place above the falls where they had camped on the way down they decided to stop for the night. The air was cool and smelled of earth, and moss, and wet leaves. The wet branches of the trees continued to drip long after the rain had stopped.

Once again the first thing they wanted was a fire and it took a real effort to get one started. Jed was disgusted with himself for forgetting to bring the firebox. They cuddled under their sleeping furs and Beth silently prayed that whatever was bothering Jed, would be worked out by God for their good. It was morning before they knew it.

Paddling up stream again didn't seem as hard now with Beth getting used to the easier rhythm Jed was setting. They would be home before the day was gone.

*****

Earlier, as Ben watched Jed and Beth pull away from the Willow trees and head down river, he realized that he was alone for the first time since Jed had joined him. He didn't like the feeling.

Ben looked toward his empty hut and thought about which project he wanted to work on first. He knew that keeping his mind and hands busy would make the time go faster. It was easy to care for the horses now that the barn was in use. He checked the chickens and fed them.

One of the hens was acting strangely dragging her wings and making a curious sound. She flew at his hand when he reached to remove the two eggs from the nest. "Well, look at you," he said. I think she has started to sit on those eggs to hatch them, he thought. I better go see if Beth has saved some fresh ones in the hut. He found a bowl with four eggs and brought them out carefully tucking them under her as she plumped her feathers to cover all of them. "You silly hen, this isn't spring. It is fall! Don't you know that you are supposed to hatch your babies in the springtime? Now I know what project I will work on. I am going to make the triangle into a safe place for you and your babies, when they hatch," he said.

Ben worked all day making a wall around the triangle with rocks, at the bottom. He built a cozy hutch that was up off the ground and insulated from the cold rocks of the bluff. He made it just big enough to be comfortable, so that their body heat would warm it, in the cold months. I will leave them where they are for now. They seem content, he thought.

The next morning, as he walked past the trees, he heard sounds coming from the wolf den. When he got down and peeked in, he saw Bold One and two cute pups. Stump came trotting up at that moment bringing her a rabbit. He was wagging and looked like he was smiling.

"Are you a proud papa?" Ben asked. "You are a good provider. That is for sure. Your babies are so cute and look at the beautiful colors. They look like you Stump."

Ben knew that Stump would give the entire rabbit to the nursing female. He searched his pockets and was happy to come up with one piece of jerky for him.

"When you come home tonight, I will give you a big bowl of stew. I promise. You have earned it."

Ben went to the garden and filled two baskets with the ready produce. He quietly returned down the path without disturbing the den. Ben spent hours cleaning and packing away some of the vegetables. Others he sliced thin and hung on the cords to dry. When his snares came up empty, he started a pot of deer stew cooking on the edge of the fire. He put it back far enough that it could simmer for a long time without burning.

He wanted to go hunting. He took his gun, some jerky and a water bag. He had learned to walk quietly through the woods. As he moved along, he found himself scanning the plants and bushes as he went. Jed has taught me so well that I do that without realizing it, he thought.

Just as he looked up from a thorn apple bush, he saw a movement ahead. He froze. The big male elk was rubbing his antlers on the branches of a small pine tree. Ben brought his rifle up slowly. He held his breath and squeezed the trigger. The big elk went crashing down heavily. The huge beast lay crumpled, at the base of the pine tree. It took Ben a moment to realize that he had finally fulfilled his desire of the previous year.

He had a huge supply of meat, an excellent hide, and a set of antlers to hang in the hut. This guy is too big for me to move alone. I need to go get Ginger, he thought. He ran all the way back to the corral. Ginger came to the gate when he called her name, but princess had gotten attached to her and wanted to come with her. It took him a few minutes to bring Ginger out without letting Princess out too. He grabbed two ropes and an old scarred hide they had been using for various jobs since the sheet had worn very thin. He was excited! "Let's go Ginger," he said as he hurried into the woods.

Ginger had no trouble keeping up through the trees, but he knew it would be more difficult on the way back. The elk lay untouched. He was still amazed at the blessing God had provided. He looked at the size of the elk and it seemed bigger than Ginger. He decided to clean it right there, saving all the useful parts. He tied his old hide to its underside so he could slide it.

He was so used to fashioning a harness from his rope that it was easy and Ginger didn't object to it. They made their way through the trees slowly.

Once back, he released the elk between the outside fire pits and started the fires burning. Just as he had finished setting up his drying racks, he saw a blur of fur, trying to make off with a meal.

"You will make a wonderful fur edge on a hood for Beth," he said softly. The animal glared at him and continued to pull on the meat. Ben shot and had to shoot again before the animal was still.

As soon as Ginger had been freed of her load, he gave her scratches and led her back to the corral. He gave her some grain and special praises. He acknowledged it had been hard for her. He checked the water supply for the corral and lifted the rock for a few minutes and watched as the channel added to the pond. When he returned to the fires and meat, he knew that he would be sleeping outside to keep the fires going and to guard the meat.

He carried the weasel down near the wolf den and brought back only the fur. That's one animal that won't bother Beth's chickens, he thought. Hurrying back to protect the elk meat from any other animal that would try to have a meal at his expense, Ben cut away the section that had bite marks and threw it as far into the trees as he could.

"I don't want meat that he touched, I feel disgusted at the thought," he said out loud. After scrubbing his hands at the edge of the river, he started making thin slices. By now it was habit and he did it with speed and skill.

Soon the racks were full. He started the fat melting in Jed's big cast iron pan. As his hands worked his mind was already creating a beautiful hood for Beth as a Christmas present. He put a big roast on over the fire and pulled the stew farther to the side on the inside fire. He put the coffee pot on, noting that he had just used the last bit of ground coffee. He didn't mind that it wasn't going to be strong. It gets stronger as it sits there anyway, he thought. All that was left to do after he cleaned things up at the river was to blow air into the stomach and hang it where it would get the smoke. It would become a waterproof container.

He looked at the antlers and could almost see pictures on the wider parts; his artistic eye was at work. Sitting comfortably on his sleeping furs, beside the two small fires, Ben decided to remove the antlers and just leave a bridge of bone to keep them attached to each other. He took them down to the water and scrubbed them with sand and water. They looked pink instead of brown or white. It was because the velvet had just been removed. He put a pan of water on to boil, and added a handful of the precious salt, he ladled the water over the antlers again and again, then he placed them near the fire where they would be in the direct sun in the morning, to dry and bleach.

Stump came up with his tongue hanging out of his mouth. He flopped beside Ben and as soon as he settled down, he was asleep.

"Guess that family is wearing you out, boy," said Ben, as he petted the big brown head. He looks well fed and content, thought Ben. His pups will make good protectors for the horses if we get them young enough. I guess the mother wolf and her two sons have moved on. Bold One wouldn't be able to use the den if her mother was still around.

Ben pulled off a piece of the big roast and was pleased to find it tender. Good enough, he thought. This will be a good addition to our provisions.

With a little effort and a bit of a mess he dipped and poured the melted fat into the intestine casings for storage. He dipped a bowl of the stew he had made and enjoyed the vegetables as much as the meat.

"Thank you, God, for your provision, for all this meat for winter, and a good hide. Thank you for the pups. They will be a big help with guarding the horses when they are grown." He sat there until he finished his stew. Stump had refused to eat any. Once again his tummy was round and full. Ben scraped the weasel skin, and the elk hide. He was thrilled to have them.

The next morning he woke to rumbles and knew that it would be raining before very few minutes passed. He took several empty baskets from the hut to carry the meat in. Clean hay, piled behind the fire pit, received the rest as Ben raced against time to get it all in before it started to rain. The meat was only partially dry, and not at all ready for storage. He grabbed his sleeping furs and tossed them inside, then went back for the new skins he had stretched the day before. It started to sprinkle on him before he made it inside. He dashed back out to collect his roast, stew and coffee pot. The baskets were set near the fire pit and added wood increased the fire inside. He sat near the doorway so that he could watch the rain come down.

He looked over at the horses. They didn't seem to even notice that it was raining. They liked to be out as much as possible but he wasn't sure if it was good for the little ones to be out in the rain. He knew they would not have had cover out on the prairie with their mothers, but he set down his cup and walked to the gate and let himself into the corral. He called Ginger.

"Let's go girl," and as she followed him, so did Princess and Angel with Surprise. He put them in their stalls and gave them all fresh dried grass. When he called Buddy, he nodded his head up and down showing that he knew his name but he stood where he was under the trees. Rusty and Missy came to him and he was able to wrap an arm around each and walk them to the barn with one on either side.

Just as he got to the stall for the twins, he felt a bump on his back and Buddy was walking along right behind him. He hugged him and gave him praise and scratches.

"You knew that I wanted you to come. Didn't you? You just wanted to do it in your own time. You are my big boy aren't you Buddy?" He put Buddy in his stall and took a few minutes to rub his beautiful coat with dry grass. "You are my special boy, yes you are." He fed them all and gave them water and closed the doors. It wasn't cold inside so he left the side windows open for light and air. The gentle breeze and rain were coming from the opposite direction.

He checked on the chickens and they were fine. "I'm glad that weasel didn't hurt any of you."

When he went back in the hut, he was soaked. He pulled his leather shirt off and rubbed his hair and skin with the remnants of his old cotton shirt. The leather shirt had to be turned inside out and rubbed with rendered fat and a smooth stone. He worked hard on the seams. I like the size it is, he thought, I don't want it to shrink or get hard.

With the rain softly but steadily falling he didn't feel that he wanted to work outside. He got out his carving tools and darted out for the antlers.

Hours sped by unnoticed. Tiny curls of white collected on the mat, on his lap as he scraped and cut, creating the pictures that he saw in his mind.

Once again he was totally lost in his craft. When he looked up he saw a dim glow in the fire pit and the day had grown brighter as the rain let up.

He fed the fire and poured another cup of coffee. He was hungry. He looked at the work he had done, and it was as if he was seeing it for the first time. He knew that it was beautiful. At the base of each antler horn, stood a regal elk like the one that had worn the antlers. Above the elk flew an eagle. Pine trees, tiny but perfect in their detail, decorated the space between. Vines curled up to the tips, each leaf a small piece of art in itself. He turned the antlers around and back, studying them.

"These are for Jed, for Christmas," he said out loud although there was no human to hear him. I could put them in the back corner of Ginger's area, under all the bundles of dry grass. No, if we decide to clear that out and make it part of the hut he would see them. Then, where should I put them? He thought about it. In the barn would be good. If I had a loft full of dry grass, that would hide them. I'm going to hang them high in a tree and secure them there so they won't fall, and then I guess I better start that loft in the morning. We will need it.

The sun came up warm and bright. The river sparkled and the fall leaves still dripped rain. Ben went to the barn and let the horses out. He checked the chickens and gave them fresh water and grain. The hen was sitting on her nest, half asleep.

"You will be a good little momma won't you?" He said, as he slowly offered her his hand with some grain in it. She gratefully ate some of it, but didn't jump down. "Keep sitting little momma, Beth is going to be so pleased and excited!"

Ben returned to the barn and started pegging the heavy split logs into place as he and Jed had planned. He put in all the uprights first so they would be there to support the loft beams when he was ready for them. It was not too difficult to construct with all the wood already inside, notched and cut to the right lengths. For the heaviest beams he used a rope tossed over the support beams of the roof. He lifted first one end and then the other.

By late afternoon he was actually standing on a narrow strip of loft floor. He stopped to eat and then went back to pegging the flooring into place. By evening he had to stop to make a ladder. The floor of the loft was about to cover the place where he was able to climb up using the stall wall. The ladder and loft floor were finished as it started to grow dark the next night. He praised God for the help with the barn, and thanked him as he gathered the horses in.

Stump came to the gate of the corral and Ben let him in. He nuzzled Ginger and gave her a lick when she lowered her face to sniff him. Then he visited each of the horses.

"Are you making sure they are all here and fine?" asked Ben. Stump wagged and jumped up on a bundle of grass and lay there panting and wagging. "Do you miss Jed and Beth? I sure do. They should be home soon, maybe tomorrow."

The horses had gotten used to Stump even though he carried the smell of the wolves on him. He always greeted them gently and had never been something to fear. Ben wondered how they all knew that he would not harm them.

Work on the loft continued the next day and by afternoon all the boards were in place. Ben had planned to start cutting grass for bundles as soon as it was complete, but he knew that the grass was still damp.

The elk meat was stiff but not as dry as he thought it should be to store in the cache so he made sure there was air circulating between all the pieces and left the baskets in the heat at a safe distance behind the fire pit inside. He looked around at the pleasant little hut and realized just how blessed he was. God had given him so much and in his mind he included Jed and Beth and all the animals. He saw the colors of the drying vegetables and bright pumpkins on their bed of dried grass. He felt much joy that his little hut was so inviting and filled with provisions for the winter.

He had walked to the river intending to go fishing but changed his mind. He reached down and touched the clay at the water's edge. I am going to try to plaster a small area behind the fireplace, he thought. If it stays on and gets hard, then I will do more. He got a watertight basket and filled it with the soupy mud. He cut grass into short lengths and mixed it into the mud. This should do it, he thought. He carried the basket into the hut and very unceremoniously started to smear it on the wall, filling in between the branches with wads of grass dipped in the clay. He made a patch about three feet wide and two feet high.

Now I hope that doesn't just become a big mess, he thought. He took the basket back down to the river and cleaned it thoroughly, leaving it upside down on the gravel to dry, then peeled off his clothes and jumped into the cold water for a quick swim and scrub.

CHAPTER TWELVE   BACK AND GLAD OF IT

Ben was sitting on the bank with three fish beside him and just pulling in another when Jed's canoe came into sight. He jumped and waved as if he thought they needed help finding the place.

"Hello. How was the trip? Boy, I am glad you are back! Beth, did you have a nice visit? Did you run into rain? We had rain here, lots of it."

"Hey Ben, calm down. We are glad to be back. We missed you, too. The trip wasn't the same without you," said Jed as he hugged Ben.

Beth started out of the canoe cautiously. It was then that Ben noticed how overloaded that canoe was. It was riding very low in the water. Beth started to step out but shrieked as it wiggled.

"Ben, we are so glad to be home, but it was nice to visit. You should see how big the twins are!" she said as he held the canoe steady while she stepped out. She also gave him a big hug.

"What have you been doing while we were gone? We could see that you weren't exactly working hard, when we came around the bend," said Jed grinning. Beth laughed.

"I'll show you what I have been doing after we get this thing unloaded before it sinks. Did you buy out the entire store?" asked Ben. "No, but we got good value for our trade goods. This stuff is heavier because the rain has soaked into the hides. Sam gave me an old slick that I have under the hides so nothing in the packs got wet."

"Beth, go ahead and go inside, Honey. We will bring everything. You are tired." She was grateful and did as he suggested. She was surprised when she went in, to see the overflowing baskets of drying meat. I can see that Ben will have a story to tell, she thought.

She put some water on to heat in a pan and added some of the herbs hanging nearby. She wanted a cup of hot tea. It was then that she noticed the plaster patch on the wall. Gently she touched it. It was still damp and cool to the touch, but felt hard. What a good idea to do that. It will be lighter in here and cleaner, she thought.

As soon as Beth was in the hut, Jed handed Ben a bundle and asked him to hide it under the grass in the back part of the barn. "It is a present for Beth," explained Jed. Ben hurried away and returned quickly so that he would not be discovered. They carried the rest of the bundles in the front door of the hut and sat them down on a mat near the fire.

"The first thing I want to do, after we do the loft, is to make a table with stools or benches. It was so nice to sit at a real table at Tom's house. It would be good to have chairs to sit on and not the floor," said Jed.

"Jed that is something I just haven't found time to do, but I've thought about it many times.

"Show me what you brought. This is like Christmas!" Beth sat on the mat sipping her tea and looking content as she watched Jed line the big bags of sugar, flour, coffee and a smaller one of salt, in a neat row on the little table that Ben had created against the back wall.

"We have two lamps, one for in here and one for the barn, and extra wicks with enough lamp oil to last a long time," said Jed, as he held one of them up for Ben to inspect. We have a scythe, a sickle, a wood plane and I brought nails. Both of these bags are nails and another hammer. All of our stuff coming back was heavier than I anticipated. That's why the canoe rode so low. Sam really liked the cradle and he wants two more in the spring." Jed winked at Ben to indicate they were for credit for supplies for the new house. They both were having fun, trying to keep their secret. Ben's nod was so slight that it was unnoticed by Beth.

"I brought back a treasure, too," said Beth. "I have two yeast balls, to use for bread in our new oven. Gentle Fawn gave me one and Rose gave me the other and three bread recipes! She gave me the instructions for soap too."

"That's great Beth, and that reminds me. I have some elk roast here and some deer stew if you are hungry. If you want to wait a bit, I caught four fish that I was going to put on the fire."

"I'll wait for the fish," said Jed.

"Me too," said Beth.

"I think I'll go check on the animals," said Beth. "I missed them. I kept thinking about them as if they were our children. Have you seen Stump today?"

"Yes, he was here earlier." As they stepped out the front door, Beth and Jed both noticed the change in the triangle.

"You have added onto the triangle, and put rocks all the way around the new wall! Is that for my chickens?" Beth asked.

"Yes, and I have made a cozy winter coop for them. That isn't the only surprise. When you check your chickens, you will find that you have a little momma sitting on six eggs! She is so vigilant that she doesn't even want to get down from her nest when she needs to eat. This morning I fed her grain from my hand and she ate sitting on the nest."

"I'm so excited! I have to go see right now," said Beth. She hurried over to the pen and peeked inside. "Look at that little darling. She is so sweet."

"Not very sweet," said Ben. "She will peck you if you reach in there. She is protective of the eggs."

Jed stood back and watched her with a big smile on his face.

"Does anyone know how long eggs take to hatch?" he asked, but no one answered. "Fine farmers we are. Guess we will have to just wait and see," said Jed.

"I do think they are supposed to hatch babies in the spring, but she doesn't seem to know that," said Ben. "That's why I got busy and made the pen up close to the bluff out of the wind. If it gets extremely cold, we can heat the coop with rocks from the fire."

"How would that work?" asked Beth.

"I left room under the coop to slide them. That's not all I did. Let's get the fish started and then we can all go to the barn." Ben strung the cleaned fish up high enough that they would take a little while to cook. "There that should do for now, so let's go. I have something there to show you."

Jed couldn't believe his eyes, when he saw the loft in place.

"It is good that you brought the nails, I ran so low that there are places we need to reinforce, but at least it is basically up."

"It is more than just up! Ben you did a fantastic job, in such a short time! We will have fun cutting the grass to fill it. We can add nails tomorrow and then go cut grass and gather grain if it is dry enough. It must have been very difficult to raise the beams all alone."

"It was, but it was fun to see it take shape."

"I want to visit the horses first but then let's go down to the garden, said Beth. I want to see how it is doing." She was smiling broadly as she approached each animal in the corral. Ginger came to her and Princess hurried and nudged her hand for attention. She gave hugs and pats to each one. "Did they all eat well? Princess seems like she has grown in just the few days we were gone."

"Yes they all ate well. I just took a big pan of mash out to the corral and one smaller one and went from baby to baby until everyone was full. They had to wash their own faces in the pool. I didn't take time for that.

Now, to the garden but let's stop at the hut first and I'll check the fish and get some jerky," said Ben. He turned a little bit so they wouldn't see the smile he was trying to hide. He pulled the fish aside and dropped them in the big frying pan. We can finish those when we get back, he thought. He was excited to show Beth and Jed the new residents of the den. He brought out a basket and his rifle. "I'm ready now," he said, as they walked down the path toward the garden. Ben stopped at the pine trees and peeked under, but he was disappointed to see that the den was empty. How can that be, he wondered. The pups are too young to go hunt. She wouldn't move them away just because I came here, would she? She knows me. She isn't afraid of me. Where could she have gone? Ben didn't give away his secret. He continued on down to the garden, where Beth used a basket, to carry several ripe tomatoes and two large green peppers.

"These will go great with the fish," she said.

Stump came bounding up barking and wagging. He was glad to have everyone back together. He jumped up against Jed and nearly knocked him backwards. He was a little gentler with Beth, but just as enthusiastic. Then he greeted Ben also with a bark and half howl that surprised all of them and made them laugh. Stump was so excited. He dashed ahead on the path and then back to them, back and forth all the way to the hut. When they started in the front door, he disappeared around the side. He stood in the middle of Ginger's old area whining and wagging. There curled up in the far corner near the open big door, were Bold One and the two pups. She had moved them, but not farther away. She had brought them here where she knew they would be safe! Ben was as astonished as anyone. Beth squealed with delight. "Oh I want to hold one! I wish she would let us." Jed looked in over the bottom door and smiled.

"I think it is probably best if we let her get used to being that close before we do anything else. How long has she been there?"

"Jed, I think she must have moved them while we were in the barn talking," said Ben. "I thought that I would show you the pups in the old den. That's why I took the jerky."

"I don't believe it. We have a wild wolf in the same house with us. I don't know if I am going to be able to sleep a wink," said Jed. "She could sail right over that door the way Stump does."

"Jed, don't be silly. Why would she want to do that? She has her babies and they are cozy and warm. If it makes you feel better, we can quietly close the top door at night."

"Beth, you are so trusting."

"She is beautiful, and so are the pups," said Beth. "They look like her, and Stump. They are a wonderful blend."

"Let's give Stump a fish for her," said Ben. He handed Stump the biggest one, and opened the front door. Without the bottom door open, Stump took it to her by going around to the side door and placed it between her front paws, then turned around and bounded in beside Ben with no effort at all.

"See what I mean," said Jed.

As they all sat around the fire eating the fried fish, and fresh vegetables, Stump lay close to the side door. He had eaten some of Ben's fish and a big piece of jerky. Ben told the story of the big elk that he had hunted. He elaborated on how he got it home and had to bring it in because of the rain, but didn't mention that it had been a big male with gorgeous antlers. He felt the teeth in his pocket and was proud of what he had accomplished while they were gone. With the weasel fur only partially processed and hidden in the bundles of grass, he thought that Christmas would be special again, but it would be hard to keep his secrets that long.

The next day, Beth tried one of the bread recipes the women had shared with her. It was her first time using the oven. It had held up well in the rain.

When all three recipes had been tried, they found that they liked one better than the others. Having a loaf of bread made meals seem complete. They had all missed it. Now she could bake other things and planned cakes, pies and cinnamon rolls for the cold months ahead.

As the days went by, the nights grew colder, and the half-wolf pups got bigger and more trusting. They would come to the door and gently take a small morsel from an extended hand. The mother, Bold One, had become quite friendly. She would actually peek in the door sometimes or come outside where one of them was working and lay a short distance away. Beth would talk to her and she would wag her tail.

Ben and Jed worried about the horses and thought it unwise to have a den of wolves around, but neither of them wanted to suggest getting rid of them. Without anyone knowing it, the smell of the horses was marking those particular horses as part of their pack. The smell of the wolves so near was something the horses had grown used to from Stump's coat.

The first snow was a light dusting that crunched from the cold when they stepped on it. Beth had transferred the mother hen and her six chicks the week before, into the cozy coop near the hut. The other hen and rooster were there too, but the momma resented them. She would peck at them if they came near her or the chicks. It became necessary to divide the roost and pen down the middle. A small slate covered bin next to the door made feeding them easy. It took several days of team spirit, but the sickle and scythe had made gathering the grass and grain easier, and with all three of them working they had the loft full of bundles of hay and the grain box in the barn was full. Jed had gathered a big basket of the wild oats for the hut. He wanted that with syrup or honey for breakfasts. The garden was resting until spring with all of its treasures properly cared for and stored. A new supply of maple syrup would be boiled down and stored, when their containers held enough of the golden sap. They had tapped three trees.

Beth had gathered a basket of withered chokecherries, and was boiling them to see what color they would make for a dye. She had made a dress from the white cotton and wanted to give it some color. She was planning shirts for Jed and Ben. The dye from the hickory nut husks would make them a nice dark tan. The cotton was easy to dye and her dress took on a soft, reddish brown. She was happy with the results.

She had used their biggest kettle on the outside fire to try her soap recipe. When it was nearly complete she had added a concentrated batch of mint tea to scent it. The soap was tan and strong. It made her skin itch. She decided that the next time she would use more fat and less lye. Also when the spring flowers were abundant, she wanted to make more soap and scent it with them.

As winter set in hard, Ben and Jed were already making plans for spring projects. Ben wanted to dig a well. They talked about its location and how they could line it. The next day they headed for the lake area, taking their guns and telling Beth they were going hunting.

"We have extra mouths to feed now," said Jed. "The pups will need lots of meat. They are growing fast." Both men knew without saying a word that they would be cutting logs for most of the day. They were making good progress. The house would not be such a big job if they could get all the logs cut ahead of time. As they worked they planned the rooms and how the roof would be supported. It would be a large rectangle that was living area and kitchen; the back portion of the cabin would be divided into two small bedrooms. The fireplace would be large and used for heat and cooking.

It was past midday when they heard movement in the brush. They both picked up their guns and pointed them in that direction. Out from under the trees came Stump and Bold One, followed by Beth.

"I thought so!" she said. "You are not hunting! You are starting a cabin. Why didn't you want me to know?"

"We wanted it to be a surprise," said Jed.

"You must be starving by now. I brought you some lunch."

"Oh Beth, we wanted to surprise you and have it closer to completion before you discovered it. It will stand on the hill that you picked and you will have a big fireplace and two bedrooms! I have made arrangements to get two big windows for the front from Sam in the spring. Are you pleased?" Jed was so excited that he was talking and laughing.

"Of course I am pleased, but I meant the hill for Ben. This is his place. We need to find a place of our own. We can't just build on his land."

"This is your place Beth. I don't want you to ever move. We are a family," said Ben.

"Oh Ben, I feel so lucky to have Jed and you. I love you both so much. Ben you are the brother that I never had. Now, show me what you are planning. We can all celebrate by eating together on the grass."

Jed took her hand and walked with her to the top of the hill. He showed her the rocks that marked the corners. He led her in to the area of the planned house, through the intended front door. He pointed to the line in the dirt that would be the wall to their bedroom.

"Will this be the baby's room?" she asked. "If you work hard, it should be ready just in time."

"Baby! A baby? Oh Beth, you didn't tell me! A baby is coming, Ben!" he shouted. "Can you believe it? We are going to have a baby!" Jed danced around and hugged her tight and swung her around in a circle.

"Congratulations Beth. That is wonderful news," said Ben. "When is the baby coming?"

"Well I'm not sure but I think the end of May or first part of June."

"That means we better get a move on and cut wood every decent day we get. It would be nice to have the cabin done before the baby arrives."

"Beth you couldn't have picked a better way to tell me. I will always remember this day. Honey, after we eat, I want to take you back to the hut so that you can rest. You still aren't as strong as you should be."

"First", she said, "let's sit and thank the Lord for all that we have, and then we can eat our lunch and just enjoy this day."

Bold One chose a spot near Beth and Stump lay nearby. Bold One accepted small pieces of bread and meat from Beth's fingers. Without thinking about it she stroked her head and scratched her ears as she would Stumps. The men watched in awe at the way Beth had tamed her.

"She trusts you," said Jed. "But you should remember she is a wild wolf, not a dog."

"Jed, she doesn't know that. She loves me and follows me wherever I go. When Stump follows you and Ben, she comes with me. I feel safe with her around. I know that she would protect me if I needed it. Remember her mother did once, with that black wolf. She attacked her mate for me."

"I don't think he was her mate. I think he was a loner that wanted to join her pack. She must have preferred Stump."

"Well Ben, it is sure easy to see that Bold One picked him for the father of the pups. They look more like him every day. I wonder sometimes where Bold One's mother has gone with the other two."

"Now it is time for you to go back and rest. I am taking you back and no arguments," said Jed laughing. I want you to take good care of our son."

"It could be a girl you know," she said smiling, as she linked her arm through his and handed him the basket to carry.

Ben was smiling at the warm feeling that existed between them. He lay back on the grass and looked up at the treetops. The wind was blowing the clouds past so quickly that it gave Ben the feeling that he was moving. He closed his eyes and thought how sweet it would be to have a child around. His mind turned to God. He prayed for God to bless Beth and strengthen her and give her a healthy baby.

"Father, bless our efforts to build the cabin and let it always be filled with joy and love, and God, please prepare a Christian mate for me."

Already he felt a pang of loneliness at the thought of Jed and Beth and the new baby here in the cabin. He would be alone again in the hut. Ginger lived in the barn now. He wouldn't even have her for company. You're being silly, he scolded. It only takes a few minutes to walk to the hut from here. I will see them every day.

Jed was back quickly.

"Hey little brother, are you napping? We have wood to cut!"

"I'm awake. Let's get some more logs cut before it gets any colder. The wind is picking up. I think we are going to get snow tonight."

Ben was right. The horses were stomping in six inches of snow and loving it when they were let out of the barn the next morning.

After cleaning the stalls and putting down new hay, Jed told Ben about his idea to make a wagon that Ginger or Angel could pull.

"I will need it to get the windows."

"Do you think we can fix the broken wheel or should we try to make a three wheeled one?" asked Jed.

"I think that the three wheeled cart would be a good idea. We can shape it so that it pulls like a travois. If we make it solid enough, it will be useful for hauling all sorts of things."

"If we work with her, we can teach Angel to pull it. That way while you are gone getting the windows, in the spring, I can use Ginger to pull the logs to the hill near the cabin site," offered Ben.

"It is sure worth a try. Not to mention that we would be able to move the growing pile of manure down to the lake, to the garden area. It would be nice to get it down where it would be useful and away from here. The bigger they get, the more there will be."

"Yes that is true," laughed both men.

Ben checked the boards they had left in a pile in the back of the barn. "We will have to cut some wood for the sides, but we have an axle, and enough wood for the base. The tongue parts are there in that pile, with the other metal parts," he said.

"Let's check on Beth to see if she needs help with anything before we start it," said Jed.

The wagon went together far easier than they thought possible. They cut the axle to a width that would be more manageable for one horse on the rough terrain. Another day was needed to cut the sides and haul them from the woods back to the barn area. Ginger pulled the wagon without hesitation but they soon realized that the trail they had been using would need widening. Several huge rocks had to be leveraged out of the way, and two small trees were cut off at ground level to allow the wagon to pass over them.

That night they pushed the wagon into the back area of the barn they had reserved for tools and equipment. They looked at it with grateful, happy hearts, knowing that once again, God had provided exactly what they had needed to do the job.

Beth came out to the barn to see how the work was going. She liked the little three-wheeled wagon but said she did have one problem with it. Now that they had used the wheels, they would need to build new drying racks.

"That's not a problem," said Ben. "We cut two small trees from the wagon path and they will be easy to cut up to form racks. We can do it this evening. That way they will be ready when we need them."

Just as they headed back toward the hut they heard growling and Jed hollering. Ben and Beth hurried to the partially open big side door where Bold One had made her bed. Jed was sitting in the hay, laughing while the pups pulled on his pant legs with all their might. When they hurried in, he explained that they had caught his pants and pulled him off balance. He had hollered when he landed in the hay.

"They are going to make holes in my pants!" he said. "They sure are playful and strong. I think we better give them an old piece of hide and some big bones for toys." Beth reached down and picked up one of the pups and it squirmed, wiggled and licked her face.

"They aren't afraid of us at all. This one is a rambunctious boy. The other one is a girl. She is gentle. I like her better." She put him down and picked up the female. The pup snuggled into her arms and was content to be held. "See what I mean. I think I want to name her Sunshine."

"That's a good name for her. What do you want to call him?" asked Ben.

"What do you think of the name Rascal?"

"I think it is perfect. It fits him." Beth carried Sunshine outside into the cold breeze and walked over to Bold One.

"We have named your babies. This is Sunshine and your little boy is Rascal." She rubbed the big wolf's ears and lowered her baby for a lick and a sniff. Bold One followed her back inside and gathered her pups to feed them.

Late one afternoon Stump and Bold One were both gone hunting. Beth had been given the trust of Bold One and she left the pups without concern. Ben and Jed returned for a quick lunch. They had been in the woods cutting logs again. They all heard a rumbling in the distance that sounded like thunder. It grew louder. They could feel a hammering vibration in the ground. It was then that they realized that they were lucky to be on this side of the river. A buffalo stampede was in progress on the other side.

"That has to be buffalo," said Jed. "I wonder what frightened them."

"I'm going to climb up to the top and take a look," Ben said, over his shoulder as he hurried out. He scrambled up the side of the bluff. The fastest route of toe and handholds was familiar to him now.

When he reached the top, he couldn't believe his eyes. As far as he could see was rolling dust and running buffalo. His heart lurched as he thought of Stump and Bold One. If they were out there, they might have been caught in that, he thought.

"Father, please protect them," he said out loud. He climbed down slowly.

"I saw buffalo running. It is a huge herd! They cover the prairie as far as I could see. I can't believe there are so many. They won't stop running for a long time, but when they do they will be exhausted. It would be easy to shoot one."

"Let's go right after the dust settles. We can take Ginger and the wagon to bring it back." Jed hurried in the bedroom to get more rifle shells. He brought out a couple of water bags and went to the river to fill them. The firebox was prepared too.

"Let's take our sleeping furs and a tent and the coffee pot with some coffee; just in case we have to stay there tonight," said Beth. "I'll take care of the chickens. We should give the pups some jerky to entertain them until Bold One comes back."

"Beth, I think you should stay here. I don't think you should be doing so much right now. Besides, the horses will need you," said Jed.

"Jed that is silly. I am healthy and the horses can go in the barn when they are ready. We can feed them some grain before we leave and throw extra bundles of hay down. They will be fine until we come back. I'll go check to make sure the pond is full." She hurried out the door before he could object further.

"She knows her own mind!" said Jed. She came back leading Angel with the foal following.

When Ben realized that the buffalo hunt was turning into an event, he suggested they wait and leave early in the morning.

"That's a good idea," said Jed. "That dust may hang over the prairie for a couple days. We don't need to rush.

CHAPTER THIRTEEN   THE BUFFALO AND A BOULDER

When the morning dawned bright and clear, the day found them already up and preparing the gear for their undertaking. The air smelled like dust. Bold One had returned just as it grew dark. They were talking excitedly over coffee, but Stump was still not home when they headed out. Ben had a bad feeling in the pit of his stomach. He was really concerned. It was worrisome for him to be gone all night.

"God, please protect Stump," he said softly.

They had taken care to see that all the animals would have plenty of food and water, enough for several days. They had closed the side door, putting a large rock in the opening. Another one held it from opening back up more than just the space Bold One would need to come and go. It would be a little colder, because the fire would be out with no one there to tend it.

The sound of the hooves passing had quieted in the night, but a heavy layer of dust still hung on the horizon.

They set out at a slow easy pace, in the direction the buffalo had gone. There was no grass left. The running buffalo had destroyed it. Far in the distance they could see a dark line of brown. The huge heard had now stopped running but some were still agitated and milling around enough to keep a blanket of dust hanging just above their backs.

Ginger and Angel were led to the trees along the river to drink and eat grass while they all took a break.

"We need to be careful. They would be easy to spook again. They are still nervous," said Jed.

After they ate, Jed lovingly picked Beth up and sat her on a piece of leather on Ginger's back. She nickered, and blew a greeting as Beth leaned forward and hugged her neck and scratched her ears.

"You are such a good girl, Ginger." Angel crowded closer, wanting to get in on the attention, so Beth leaned over and scratched her too.

"Ben, look. Stump is coming!" She knew he had been worried. They all had been.

Stump was coming toward them from the direction of the herd. He must have been following them. Ben knelt and hugged the dusty fur of Stump's neck.

"I am so glad that you are safe and sound." He turned away from Jed and Beth. The tears of relief that spilled from his eyes embarrassed him.

"Thank you Father," he said as he handed Stump a piece of jerky and wiped his cheeks quickly with the back of his hand. He was unaware that his tears had mixed with dust and he had a large brown smear on each cheek.

Moving slowly, they eased close enough to make it possible to see individuals in the herd they saw a young bull calf that was limping badly. Not far away a cow stood spread legged and exhausted. She could go no further.

"Which one do you want to try for," asked Jed?

"Both," said Ben.

"I'll take the cow for the big hide. You aim for the calf for the good meat." Jed nodded.

"The less we talk the better. Beth, please stay here and bring the horses when we are ready." He tied Angel's lead to the back of the wagon. "Just direct Ginger and Angel will follow along." She stood beside Ginger patting her neck as the two men cautiously approached their chosen targets.

At a hand signal, both men raised their rifles and fired. The hunt was over that quickly. Ben used a second bullet, just to be sure. The sound of the rifles started the herd moving away, running again.

"This time they won't go as far or as fast. They are about run out," said Jed. He looked at the cow on the ground and said, "Good shot Ben. I don't think you would have needed the second bullet."

They had started the job of cleaning them when Ben hollered for Jed to come quick.

"Look at this! We got two for one." The nearly full term calf that the cow carried was a bonus that neither of them had thought of. The leather would be the softest possible, and an extra warm blanket for Beth's baby, and the meat would be very tender. The meat of the bull calf was a struggle to leverage up on the wagon. They laid the tiny calf with it. The cow was rolled onto a travois and tied, but every time Angel felt the tug of the heavy weight, she stopped.

"It is too heavy for her. She has never pulled anything but the lightest loads,' said Jed.

"Somehow we have to get some of the cow off the travois," said Beth. They ended up skinning the cow and cutting the meat into sections. One half was rolled in its own hide and placed on the travois. The rest was made into bundles for their backs and the backs of the horses. The heavy heads and lower legs of the buffalo were left in the prairie dust to feed other creatures.

Finally they started for the river and the trees beside it. Ginger and Angel were allowed to drink and eat, while Ben and Jed cleaned themselves and the wagons as much as possible. After the short break they headed home, with more meat waiting to be processed than had ever been in camp at one time. Beth was wondering what she would do with the unborn calf hide. Maybe I'll stitch around the edge of it with yarn. I think I should trim it into a rectangle first. Yes that would leave pieces to make little booties for her feet. At the moment she was thinking it would be a girl.

Beth had remembered to feed the firebox, so getting the fires going outside the hut was not as difficult as it might have been.

The pups came out to greet them, followed by Bold One. The horses came to the fence to acknowledge their return. The pups climbed up on the travois and sniffed at the raw hide. Beth picked them up one on each arm and carried them back to their area and closed the side door. She opened the front door of the hut wide so that Bold One could enter and jump over the half door if she wanted to be with them.

"Oh! Oh my! Ben! Look! The roof is ruined! I guess it is a good thing that we were not here when the boulder went through! This could have killed one of us!" Ben and Jed hurried over to look inside at the tangle of branches and dirt that used to be the middle of the hut. The center pole was crushed to the ground by a huge boulder, five feet in diameter.

"The vibration of the stampede must have loosened it," said Jed.

"I think I better climb up and be sure there are no others ready to fall," said Ben. He took one of his spears that lay near the door where it had been knocked by the debris. He headed up his usual way. The hole left by the boulder was large. He used the spear to poke around in the area above the hut, but nothing else large seemed loose. A few pebbles here and there dribbled down but nothing of concern. He made his way over to the area above the corral and barn and checked there.

"Thank you, my Father, that no one was injured." He praised God as he looked down for the first time at the damage to the hut. The center of the roof was destroyed. He would have to rebuild it quickly. It was winter. They needed shelter.

As they stood beside Beth, she calmly lifted her voice and praised God for the buffalo meat they had and that they had gotten it without anyone getting hurt. She thanked God that Stump had returned to them safely, and that they had all been gone when the boulder went through the roof of the hut.

Next she turned to Jed and Ben and told them to unload the meat as close to the fires as they could and take the wagon and travois to the river and scrub them. She handed them a big bar of the strong soap, and a brush she had made for scrubbing. For the first time ever, she had to take charge. The men seemed numb and did as she said unquestioningly.

When they had Ginger and Angel in the corral eating fresh hay and the wagon and travois cleaned and back in the barn, she asked them to carry the sleeping furs to the barn and to make a place for them to sleep for the next few days. They piled their arms full and once again followed her instructions.

She sliced meat as fast as she could. She knew that the food stored in the hut would be fine for now, but getting to it would be difficult. She stepped just inside the hut far enough to reach a two pans. The roof looked like the rest of it would come down with the slightest disturbance. She wondered how they would get that huge boulder out of there.

When Jed and Ben came back from the barn, she asked Ben to crawl into the bedroom through the window and bring out any extra hides and bedding. We will have to work out here processing and guarding the meat. We might as well be warm and comfortable. Once again he didn't question the wisdom of her words.

She cut a big roast from the bull calf and put it over the fire. She reached in beside the wall with Ben's spear and rolled a pumpkin out the door. She broke it open scraping the seeds onto a rock and covered them with a piece of stained cloth that she had used for a potholder many times. It would do to keep the birds off. After the skin of the pumpkin was plastered with clay and placed near the fire to bake, she continued to slice meat.

Jed sat down beside her after smoothing out the hides. He looked worried.

"Beth, I can't think of any way to move that big rock. It is too heavy for us, even if we use Ginger and Angel."

"We will think of a way," she said, "but right now we are all tired and have lots of meat to cut up and hides that will need scraping. We are fortunate that we have the barn to use." Ben came up and noticed Jed's glum face.

"Cheer up, big brother. I have a plan. What do you think of this idea? If we pull the roof of the main room down and use the wood to extend the walls out front. We can use the boulder as a starting point and build forward from there. We can cut a new door to the bedroom in the front corner. The door to the wolves is far enough forward that it will be fine."

"You mean build out in front of the rock and leave it there?" Jed asked.

"Sure."

"Once we get the broken roof off, we will be able to safely reach the caches in the back corners. Maybe we can figure out a way to keep rain out of them and leave them right there." All we need to do is move the front wall forward and shape a back wall in front of the boulder and put a new roof on."

"Is that all?" Jed said with a frown on his face. "Ben, you always make everything sound so easy. Don't you ever get tired?"

"Sure I do, but this plan has another good point to it. I figure that it probably was Indians hunting that started that stampede. If we build the way I suggest, the back section will give us a place to slip into where we won't be found, if they ever come here. We can hang a hide against the back door of the bedroom to conceal it. It will open to that area around the rock and to the bluff. It would be possible to slip in there and hide, or to keep going and climb up the bluff."

"You are amazing," said Jed. "You figured all that out while we were working! Ben, you know that I'll be glad to help," said Jed apologetically.

"Actually," Jed continued, "I have been thinking of putting a shed on the back of our cabin when we build it, with a room underneath. It would be good for storage and to hide in if it ever is necessary. From that room we could have a tunnel that leads into the woods behind."

"Great minds think alike!" said Ben and they all laughed.

"See," said Beth, "you will end up with a place that is bigger and better than the first one. Ben I am so glad that you are taking this the way you are. Nothing discourages you."

"We are doing a fast job here," said Ben. "We have talked our way through most of the bull calf. Look at all the meat. We will need more racks to dry all this. I think I will go cut branches while you two keep cutting meat." He came back in a little while with his arms full of long straight branches, freshly cut. Jed helped tie them together with raw sinew. "They will be stable and strong when that dries hard," said Jed.

"Do you really think the Indians would come here and find us Ben?" Beth asked.

"Now he was sorry he had made such an issue of his plan. He could have told Jed without worrying her. She looked tired and drawn. She had been up since dawn, helping to prepare, and then following the herd and now helping with the meat. Jed saw the same thing Ben did. He really wished that Ben had not said that.

"Is that meat done? Let's eat. I'm starving." Beth knew that his animation was intended to change the conversation and mood and she tried to respond. She handed him a piece of the pumpkin first with a spoon and said that she knew that he was eager to eat his vegetables. They ate with little conversation and when the meal was over; Jed took her hand and insisted that she go with him. He tucked her into her sleeping furs in the barn. She was on a soft bed of hay, comfortable, warm and feeling loved and cared for. The new lantern hung high on a beam. He turned the wick low and the lantern gave a cozy glow.

"Sleep well, Beth," he said softly and then tenderly kissed her good night and went out closing the door.

A few minutes later Jed returned to the campfire and the task of cutting the slices of meat to dry.

"This cow alone would be enough meat for all winter," said Jed. "I hope we can dry it all before the weather changes," he said. "If it snows and then thaws that could be bad. It could ruin all of this and the meat in the exposed caches."

"Jed, the weather will hold, and we will have it all cut up by morning. All we will do tomorrow is watch it dry and feed the fires

181

and rest. It is Sunday. I looked at the calendar sticks before we left. I won't be able to get to the Bible to read, though, until we get the roof off the hut. I hope the Bible wasn't damaged," said Ben.

"If we have to, we can pile the dried meat in the barn on hay until we get caches dug for it," said Jed trying to be more optimistic.

"We have plenty of room in there to dig a couple new caches," Ben suggested. He was trying hard to stay positive.

"Did anyone give some of this meat to Bold One and the pups?" asked Jed. "I think they would like the fresh meat instead of jerky." He took a huge bone in the side door of the hut and gave it to Bold One. He had left lots of meat on it." He came out with Sunshine in his arms. She was licking his fingers. "She is the sweetest thing," he said, with a grin. "When I came out, Rascal was pulling on a piece of meat and trying to take that bone away from his mother! Guess I better put her back and then I'll wash my hands."

Jed returned to the campfire after a trip to the river's edge just in time to see movement in the trees to the side.

"We have a visitor in the trees. A big one," he said quietly, as he picked up his rifle. He was glad that Beth was with the horses, asleep in the closed barn. The windows were closed and latched. They were safe. He couldn't quite make out the shape of the animal, but could see the reflected light of the fire in its eyes as it stared at him.

"I think it's a big cat." Ben felt his hand tense on the rifle at his side. Suddenly they heard a growl come from behind them. It was Bold One. She stood between the two men and the animal in the trees. Her hair on her back was standing tall and her growl seemed to come from the very earth she stood on. She was swiftly joined by Stump adding his growl as support beside her. The animal in the trees could be heard retreating.

"Well, what do you think of that?" said Jed. Bold One turned toward the hut and went inside to the side room, followed by Stump.

"I don't know what to make of that, but she sure is brave and so was Stump," said Ben.

"We need to take off any loose parts on that roof, before they fall and hurt her or Stump. We should do it first thing in the morning," commented Ben."

"I will be interested in checking for tracks to see what was in the woods," said Jed.

"I think it was a big cat," said Ben, "as they settled back into the job of slicing."

"I can't believe that we got so much. This hide from the cow is a beautiful strong hide. There isn't a scar on it," said Jed. "The unborn calf hide is actually fuzzy, now that it is getting dry."

CHAPTER FOURTEEN   THE ENEMY

At that moment, the pan full of grease bubbled over; sending flames into the sky. Jed grabbed at the edge of the pan with the rag that covered the pumpkin seeds, to pull it away from the fire and the scalding grease splashed into his hand and on his arm. He dropped the pan and the grease spilled into the fire and on the rocks and ground. The flames shot up high and spread to the grease spill instantly. Both men began kicking dirt onto the fire. Ben ran for the shovel and shoveled dirt over it until it was back under control. Jed stood a few feet away. His hand was bright red and starting to blister. He ran to the river and plunged it under the surface, gritting his teeth to keep from screaming out. Ben stood there not sure what to do first.

"Willow bark," Ben said out loud "and some bear grease with something to cover it? Jed, tell me what to do to help you!"

"Yes Ben. Make strong willow bark tea and add some of the dried purple flowers. Be careful of that roof. Don't bump anything. If you can't do it safely, then you know where there are some of the dry plants down by the lake," said Jed. He had spoken in a calm monotone voice that was so controlled that it was unnatural.

"I can do it!" yelled Ben. His heart was racing, Isaiah 53:5 NIV says, "By His wounds we are healed." He shouted the first words of scripture that came to his mind.

"Jesus, please help Jed. His hand is burned Lord, without your help, it will be really bad. Oh Jesus, help him. You can heal all kinds of sickness and diseases and I know you will heal him if I ask. I am asking now, Jesus, please, oh please heal him." He thought that Jed's hand might be badly scarred if it weren't properly cared for right away. He couldn't see inside the hut. It was totally black inside. He grabbed the rag. It was partially burned. He wrapped it around the end of a stick and tied it, rubbing it into a puddle of the fat that had splashed away from the fire as Jed dropped the big pan. He lit it and headed back into the hut. He held the torch low so that it wouldn't ignite any hanging branches.

Inching along slowly, he could see the dried flowers against the wall. A large branch hung at an angle barring his way. It was impossible to get to them. Then he thought of his fishing pole. It lay on the floor, knocked near the doorway. He used its tip to hook the bundle of dried purple flowers and brought them ever so carefully through the tangle. On his way out he was able to collect another pan. He poured water into it from a water bag, hastily adding some of the dried flowers. He gathered fresh willow bark and hoped that he hadn't damaged the tree badly. He had cut deeper than he intended. He looked at Jed, sitting now in the river with his back to Ben. He rushed down to check on him and to ask if the flowers were to go in the tea or to make a poultice for the burn.

"Both," Jed answered in that strange sounding voice. Ben could see that Jed was shaking from the cold water and shock. That is when Ben remembered that he was supposed to get bear grease. It was in the cache. How would he get to it? He grabbed the torch that lay on the ground still burning. He ran to the back and crawled in the window. The chickens in their pen below him set up such a racket that it caused Bold One and Stump to come barking and running to the rescue again. This time they both stood looking at Ben wondering what he was doing. He climbed down into the bedroom and was able to reach only the first cache. The second one, which held the basket of bear grease, was on the other side of the boulder. Going back out the window, he climbed up on to the bluff above the hut and began ripping off sod and branches from the caved in roof as fast as he could; without causing the whole thing to collapse. The cache top was visible from where he was, if he could figure out a way to get to it. He had cleared the corner of the roof. If he jumped down in, he wasn't sure that he could get back out with the torch and grease.

Beth came out of the darkness and appeared beside him on the bluff.

"Ben what has happened? Where is Jed?" she asked. A note of panic had entered her voice.

"What are you doing up here?" he asked. "I thought you were sleeping."

"I was until the chickens and barking woke me. Ben, what is going on?"

"We had an accident and Jed burned his hand and he is sitting in the river and I need to get the bear grease out of the cache but if I jump down in there, I won't be able to get back up."

"Ben, I can do it. After I have the grease, you can pull me up. See the rope right there hanging on the back wall. I will toss the end up to you." Without further discussion she moved to the edge of the roof and jumped down. Beth landed with her heel on a small branch on the floor and turned her ankle. She did not let on that she was injured. She jerked the top off the cache and pulled the big basket of grease out. Using a loose branch she dug a big scoop of the grease out, handing the branch up to Ben. With the basket back in the cache, she pushed the lid back into place.

"I am ready, Ben," she yelled, "I'll toss the rope up." It fell back to the floor several times before they thought to tie it to the end of the branch she had handed up to him, with the other end under her arms he was able to help her climb out. She didn't wait for Ben with the grease and a torch. She scurried down and ran to the river. Jed was shaking violently. His lips were blue.

"He will be sick! Why did you let him stay in the freezing water?" Beth yelled! Ben didn't even try to explain all that he had been doing. He thought that Jed, even though injured would know what to do, and that he would stay in control. Ben had been wrong. He could see that Jed was in bad shape. He added cold water to cool the pan of medicine a little and then he and Beth worked to strip off Jed's freezing cold, wet, leather clothing. Beth rubbed him dry with one of the furs and wrapped him in another. Ben ran and came back with their coats and more furs to bundle Jed and Beth. She too was shaking from the cold. She had gotten wet while helping Jed.

In just a few short hours, their successful buffalo hunting party had found themselves returning to a demolished roof, a threat of attack by a huge animal in the dark, a grease fire, a badly burned hand and arm and Jed had taken a deadly chill.

Ben handed a cup of the strong tea to Beth for Jed. Next he closed his eyes and raised his hands toward heaven and prayed out loud.

"Heavenly Father, we thank you for the bountiful provision that surrounds us. We thank you that you directed us out of camp so that no one was killed when the boulder fell, and we thank you that we are here together. Jesus, we praise you for all that you have done and will do for us. Thank you for the protection provided by Bold One and Stump when the animal came near.

Now we ask that you cover Jed with Your mighty healing power and give him your blessing. Jesus, please heal his hand and arm so that he will not have permanent damage. Help us to make a good and safe repair to the hut. Bless us all Lord, especially the coming baby, in Jesus name I pray." And they all said "Amen."

They were silent for a moment just watching the flames of the fire that so often was a friend and a lifesaving comfort. This time it had been an enemy.

Ben dipped the numbing flowers and soft willow bark out of the dark liquid. It was mushy.

"This will be a poultice for the burns, but first I want to smear bear grease on," said Ben.

"No, just mix the flowers into the grease," said Jed.

"I'll smear it on thick so that it will last a long while," said Ben. Jed's hand and arm were shaking, as Ben gently coated the burned area generously with the mixture.

"Jesus, the Christ, heals you," he said softly. He wrapped rabbit skins around it and tied it on with strips of the same thing. Jed's entire body was shaking again. Ben could tell that Jed was running a fever.

Beth cuddled beside him and wrapped more furs around him trying to warm him.

She had seen that her ankle was swollen and growing purple on the side. Without drawing attention to it, she pulled Jed's freezing wet shirt closer and wrapped it around her ankle. Ben gave Jed another cup of the medicinal tea to drink.

After adding wood to both of the big fires, Ben sat down and with a constant prayer on his lips and the rifle at his side; he finished cutting all the meat into thin strips. He had to make more drying racks. When the racks were pulled up close to the fire on the far side, it seemed that they were in a fenced enclosure.

He walked to the edge of the campsite and stretched the three hides. He would scrape them as soon as he could. He started to clear up and clean the area where they had worked. The four biggest teeth from the buffalo cow were in his pocket and would be added to his growing collection. He noticed how different they were from the other teeth he had.

Walking up river a short distance, he filled the water barrel with fresh, clean water. He was glad that he had been able to reach it without a problem. He set it down near Beth and offered her a cup of the fresh cold water.

Ben put on a pan of fresh water for tea and put in clover and soon transferred some of that to the pan of medicine for Jed. To the second pan he added chamomile and mint. Beth was resting now and so was Jed. Ben was thankful for that.

As morning approached Ben quietly called Stump out to lie near the meat to guard it and the sleeping people. To his surprise Bold One came out too, and joined the alert vigil. As long as those two are on guard, I know that it will be safe for me to leave. He hurried to the lake and tried hard to find wild onions. He couldn't get near the ones in the hut. He found a few but wanted more. It was harder to find them this late in the year and in the partial light of early day.

It was impossible to reach the frying pan, but he did pull out another kettle that would have to do. He chopped the onions stems and all, and added them to hot grease. He had the calf's liver sliced and ready to fry. The smell of the sizzling onions woke Jed.

"That sure smells good. What are you cooking?" "Calves liver, with wild onions for you and me, and I have three eggs that I will make for Beth." Beth raised her head.

"Yuk! I hate the smell of liver."

"That's for Jed and me. You get eggs. We still have some of the last bread you baked in our bundles, too."

"Jed, how does your hand and arm feel? That is a nasty burn. We need to be very careful to keep it clean so that you don't get an infection in it," said Beth.

"It is pretty painful. I think I need to have an infection fighter like the plant we used on your shoulder, Ben, and Stump's side, added to the poultice. Like she says Ben, I don't want to get an infection in it. Do we have any that you can get to?"

"Yes, Jed but not now; I should have most of the loose roof off by noon and then we will see what we can reach," said Ben.

"Mean time you better drink some of this tea and eat the liver and onions."

"I don't feel hungry but I will eat some. The tea tastes like it has clover added to it."

"It does. I hope that is all right," said Ben

"That's fine. It fights infection. Did you know that?" Ben nodded and stifled a yawn as he stuffed his mouth with the tender fried liver.

"You should rest for a while before you tackle that roof. You were up all night. I can play nurse and feed the animals. I see that Stump and Bold One are on guard. That is sure a good pair of friends we have." She reached over and stroked Stump and gave him a hug and did the same to Bold One. She handed each of them a piece of the drying meat and they lay together, enjoying it. Beth started to get up and let out a cry of pain. She had forgotten her ankle until she tried to put weight on it.

"Honey, what is the matter?" asked Jed with concern. Ben rushed to her side. She pushed her ankle out from the furs and was shocked when she removed the now dry shirt. It was badly swollen and dark purple all the way down under the arch of her foot.

"Honey, how did you do that?" asked Jed.

"I twisted it when I jumped down to get the grease."

"Oh Beth, I'm so sorry. You never even let on," said Ben. "I should not have let you do it. You shouldn't use that for a few days. Guess you will join Jed on the sick list. You can nurse each other." Ben dipped a rabbit hide into the icy cold river and wrapped it around her ankle with the rest of the poultice left in the pan. He knew the purple flowers would numb the pain in her ankle. He poured her a cup of the medicinal tea.

"Stay put for now while I see to the animals," he said, "and then I will find a branch you can use for a crutch." Before long he was back. He had made a crutch and padded the top with rabbit's fur. He used the shovel to further clean up the area, moving the soiled earth to the woods and filling in where needed with fresh clean dirt from under the trees.

"Next the roof," he announced as he placed his rifle beside Beth. "Don't hesitate to use that if you need to. Jed's is here, but he won't be holding anything in his right hand for a while." Beth watched as Ben climbed up the bluff to the back of the roof and started removing branches. Some he allowed to drop inside, while others he pulled loose and tossed outside the walls.

As he had predicted the night before, by noon he had the roof down. It lay in a jumble inside and out, mixed with a lot of dirt, sod and stones. The floor was covered. He circled the wall inside the hut and was able to squeeze through to reach things that had been blocked. He found the indentations in the branch that held teeth and he stuffed them all into his pocket. He brought out the plants that Jed needed from behind the fire pit and added some of the crushed plant and more willow bark and water and set the pan close enough so that it would heat. He continued to work for another hour, pulling branches out the front door and piling them neatly to the side.

"Tomorrow I will start on the rubble. Beth, all your baskets survived that were hanging around the fire pit. The tops you made kept the dried foods in and the dirt out. One is a little crushed, but it still holds the dried tomatoes. I collected all of the baskets and put them against the bluff at the back of the bedroom where they will stay dry. I was able to bring the Bible. It stayed safe on the ledge in the side wall. It had a bit of dirt on the cover, but that brushed right off." He pulled it from his shirt and placed it on the fur beside her.

"That's wonderful Ben," said Beth. She placed her palm on it as if ready to make a vow.

"Now it is time for you to rest. You have done all that you can for a little while. Come over and sit down. Have a cup of the tea you made for me this morning and a piece of the meat. I was able to hop around the racks and turn some of the meat. The ones that were closest, when the fire flared up have a smoky smell, but I think they will be useable. If you would bring out the salt later we could try rubbing some into those and it might be quite tasty that way, but not now. Right now you need to rest." Ben poured a cup of tea and sat down on one of the furs. He nibbled on a small piece of the roast. With a deep sigh, he lay back on the fur and closed his eyes.

When Beth saw that he was asleep, she got up quietly and hobbled around adding wood to the two fires. The crutch was helpful and she managed to quietly move slowly around without waking him. She gently covered him.

"Thank you Father," she said softly, "You have watched over us and I know that with you, we will be fine."

When the first few flakes of snow began to fall she decided to do what she could to protect things from the moisture. She hopped inside the hut carrying one of the heavily greased skins they had been using for utility purposes. It was difficult to believe that the mess of jumbled branches and dirt had once been the cozy and orderly hut. She took her time and made her way cautiously to the back where she had several big, empty collecting baskets piled in the corner. With the hide, she carefully covered the heavy bags of flour, sugar, coffee, and salt, and then she brought out the baskets and began piling the meat into them. She knelt near the first drying rack, making sure that she didn't fall.

Jed woke, sat up and pulled on his dry clothes noticing that they were a little tight. They had shrunk. He kissed her on the cheek and chuckled.

"Together we make one good person." He picked up both handles of the full baskets and carried them to the barn with his left arm. She started to object but then realized that his help was badly needed. As she filled the baskets, he took them two at a time. She had filled all the baskets and he had transported them to the barn and emptied them onto a pile of clean hay. It was starting to snow quite hard. They still had racks of meat hanging by the fire. It took many trips, but finally when Jed returned with two empty baskets, the last of the meat was removed and put in the barn.

"We are going to need our boots. Let's get Ben up now before he gets buried and he can bring them for us," said Beth.

Ben couldn't believe his eyes. The ground was white and so was the fur covering him.

"I have covered the dried foods in the hut, and Jed has taken the meat into the barn, but we need your help to bring our boots and the furs," Beth said. "I'll take the cups, and Jed can take the Bible. If you can bring the rest of the stuff, then we can make a small fire pit in the floor of the barn." "Yes, that's good." He replied only half awake. He gathered the furs and took those first, returning for the two pans of tea.

Ben entered the area that Bold One now called home, and rubbed his feet dry on the hay. He scratched her ears and played with the pups for a minute, then pulled his boots on. He tucked his travel shoes; he had been wearing into his waistband. "I'm taking those with me, so you guys won't use them for something to chew on," he said to the pups as he shut the big side door against the stone and propped it open just enough for Bold One and Stump to come and go. He returned for the roast and pushed hot coals into the big cast iron pot that he could now reach. Beth and Jed had been busy. They had firewood and a ring of stones ready. Ben tipped the coals onto the wood and soon a nice little fire was going.

"Ben I am sorry to ask, but would you go get some beans, a chili pepper and some dried tomatoes? We will need both water bags and bowls and spoons." Ben didn't mind. Another collection basket of meat was dumped onto the hay to save trips.

How beautiful everything was becoming as the snow outside continued to come down. One by one the horses drifted in and went to their clean stalls. Angel came in the door and walked over to Jed and rubbed her muzzle on his shoulder. He reached up with his good hand and patted her and gave her a scratch. She continued on her way to her stall with Surprise.

"She is the last one. When Ben comes back I will ask him to close the door."

When Ben stepped in the door of the barn he was met by the glow of the fire, and the light of the lantern. He put the food down near the big pot and closed the door.

"It is positively festive in here," he said.

He could see that his companions were both in pain. As soon as they were reheated, he handed Jed a cup of the tea and poured one for Beth.

"You have both done so much, but thank you for it. We should be cozy here tonight and we will leave tomorrow in God's hands." Just then they heard a scratching at the big door. Ben opened it wide enough to allow Stump, Bold One and the pups to enter. The horses stomped a bit and snorted. The wolf had never come into the barn before. Ben led Stump to a spot away from the horses in a corner. He put down some hay and told him to stay. Bold One accepted that this was the place she was to use and went there, followed by Sunshine and Rascal.

"There we are. The whole gang is here," said Jed with a little laugh.

"Beth, I checked on the chickens and they are cozy and fed. I filled their water pan and put it back away from the door. Their body heat should keep it from freezing. Now, I think we should get this mysterious meal going. What do I do first?" asked Ben. "If you direct me, I will make it. That way you can stay seated."

"Thanks Ben," said Beth, "Just rinse a couple of big handfuls of the beans and put them into the kettle with water. Put it where it will boil. When the beans get soft we can add the rest of the ingredients." They sat by the fire quietly until Ben picked up the Bible and turned to the book of Job.

"Last night it seemed we were all being tested," he said. "I thought we should read some of the book of Job while our food is cooking." He read for quite some time.

Sunshine found her way into Beth's lap and Rascal came over and tried to chew Ben's fingers as he held the Bible.

"You are a distraction, little fellow." Ben held him close with one hand while he stirred the beans with the other and then he placed the pup back with its mother.

"What should I add next?"

"Just put in a whole bunch of the tomatoes and I am not sure how hot the peppers are, so add about a teaspoon of the seeds from the hot pepper. We can always add more if we want it hotter. If you would, just cut two or three strips of the meat into bites and add that. It should be ready soon. I wish I had told you to bring a few onions from the baskets and salt." Ben went out quickly. Before she could object, he had picked up the lantern and was gone. He wasn't eager to go out into the snow again but he had realized that if he didn't transfer the squash and pumpkins they would freeze and be ruined. He bundled as many as he could carry into the old sheet and carefully placed them in the hay of the barn. It took several trips before he had all of them. When he returned the last time, he had his arms full again. He had brought the cinnamon, sugar and the wild apples along with the onions and salt she had asked for. "We are going to have a feast, because we are in a warm barn, and are together with people we love and all of this is in God's hands," he said.

He added the salt, with Beth's direction and some dried onions. Next he put a little water and a spot of grease in another pan. He cut up the apples and let them simmer.

"When they are soft we can add the sugar and cinnamon. Now I want to finish our Bible reading with Job 42:12 NIV.

"And the Lord blessed the latter part of Job's life more than the former part."

"If we have faith in Him, all things turn out for good."

Ben dished out the chili, but Jed ate very little and seemed to be in a lot of pain. Ben's concern was written on his face.

"We need to check your hand Jed. I'll be as gentle as I can." When he removed the bandage they were surprised to see that some of the burn was not as red as it had been. Jed had two big blisters, one by his thumb that ran to the center of his palm and one that ran along the back of his hand up onto his arm. The rest of the burn seemed to be cooling. Beth applied more of the grease poultice; she had added more willow bark and some more of the crushed boiled flowers. They wrapped it and gave him another cup of the medicinal tea.

"Save me some apples," Jed mumbled as he drifted off to sleep.

"You're next," said Ben. "Let me see that ankle. It looks worse!" said Ben. Beth agreed that the color looked worse but she said it wasn't as painful.

"It is still swollen some though," she said. Ben dipped a soft piece of leather into the hot medicinal tea and wrapped it around her ankle. He bunched up the hay under her foot and told her to lean back and rest.

"You were on it too much," he scolded.

"Thanks Ben, that feels a lot better."

Princess came over to Beth and lay in the hay beside her.

"She hasn't forgotten me as a substitute mother," said Beth. She wrapped her arm around the young horse's neck as she had those first few nights and they both fell asleep. Ben walked quietly over to Ginger and scratched her ears and talked to her and next he visited Buddy.

"We are going to have such good times together next summer. I can't wait to see you run full out," he said, as he ran his hand along the beautiful white coat. Each stall held precious animals that he loved and valued. The twins stood side by side. They had plenty of room if they wanted to move away, but they didn't. He hugged them both giving scratches and patted their rumps. Angel was lying in the hay with Surprise. She blew softly as he patted her and scratched her ears and neck. He smiled at the sleeping foal. He walked over to see Stump and his family and then went back to the warm furs near the fire. The chili was pulled farther from the heat and the lid put on it. He added water to it and the two pans of tea and relaxed. He too was soon asleep.

In the middle of the night, the sound of Jed's movement, trying to add wood to the fire, woke Ben. He took over.

"It is not as cozy here as in the hut," Jed whispered. "I wanted to warm the tea. My hand is hurting. I think I may have bumped it in my sleep." By the light of the fire Jed could see Beth and the young horse, cuddled together. "It looks like I have been replaced," he said, with a smile. "I have been listening to the wind for the past hour or more. We are going to have some deep drifts out there."

"I hope that everything is protected in the hut." Ben poured the medicinal tea for Jed and put some of the chamomile in his own cup.

By morning the snow had stopped coming down, but the fierce wind continued. It was bitter cold. Ben went out several times and brought in loads of firewood. He brought all the baskets of dried vegetables and sacks of flour, sugar and salt into the barn. The only food left in the hut was the dried meat in the caches.

His next trip he brought a hide in his arms. Wrapped inside were all the bundles of dried herbs and seasonings they had gathered. He remembered the buffalo hides at that moment and went out again. They had been totally hidden by the snow. He first brought the big cowhide. It was frozen stiff and hard to handle in the wind. The second trip he brought the others. He had even found his favorite stone that he used to work the fat into a hide after it was scraped. He spread them out in the empty back stall to thaw and later spent several hours scraping them, and then tacked them temporarily to the wall to dry. They would be scraped many times and rendered fat would be worked into every inch of them before they were finished.

He poured the last of the chili into a smaller pan and took two of the hot rocks from near the fire.

"I am going to check on the chickens and put these under the coop to warm them up a bit. If they get too cold I could bring the coop in here somehow. He returned with two eggs. "I think one is from yesterday. I fed them and they seem fine. The walls on the coop are thick and it is cozy inside, but I put the rocks under there anyway. Jed, I also brought the coffee and the pot. I knew that you would want some by now."

"Thanks a lot. I would like some," he said.

He had also brought the cooking pouch and basket of oats and the maple syrup. He put some of the oats on to cook. Beth was awake and Princess had gone back to her stall where she knew that fresh hay and grain would be waiting for her. Ben had filled their water baskets the night before, but now he had to melt snow to have water for them.

Buddy came over and nearly knocked the chili over trying to put his face in it.

"That isn't mash Buddy. Come on Buddy let's put you back in your stall and I will make you some mash. I guess I could make a couple of pans of mash, enough for all of you." Ben poured the two pans of tea together and added a little more willow bark and set it where it would simmer slowly. He cleaned out the biggest pan and scooped it half full of grain and added water and put it on to cook. He did the same with the tea pan. He had the cooking pouch with the oats hanging from a branch he had stabilized with stones. "I hope I can keep track of all this," he said.

Beth wiggled over without putting any weight on her sore ankle. She filled her bowl with the cold chili.

"This is what I want for my breakfast," she said. "I love this stuff, hot or cold." Ben looked at her in disbelief.

"Yup, you sure are pregnant!" They all laughed. "You know in spite of everything, I think this is fun," said Ben.

It snowed two more nights in a row. The drifts against the corral fence were waist high in places. Ben pushed his way through the snow to the hut. He wanted his calendar sticks. Beth wanted the bolt of fabric from the bedroom, her scissors and needle and thread. Jed wanted his bundle that he kept in the bedroom with his carving stuff in it. He had started a bowl and wanted to see if he could work on it. Ben knew that it was too soon but he didn't want to discourage Jed.

Ben chose the section with the tools, as far from the wolf family as possible. He created a barricade with the travois and some wood to keep them confined to that area, and then he brought the rooster and laying hen. Next he gathered the chicks in one of their biggest baskets with a lid, and put the mother hen under his coat and brought them in where they would be warmer and easier to care for. He scattered grain on the floor of their temporary pen and gave them some water.

"They seem quite happy there," observed Jed. "Just put a bundle of hay down in the corner so they can snuggle up to sleep," he said.

"The mother looks like she is checking every chick to make sure they are all there and all right," said Ben.

"Beth your chicks are not fuzzy any more. They all are getting feathers. They are a lot faster; I had quite a time catching them and getting them into the basket."

It must be early November, he thought. The marks on the sticks confirmed it.

Jed's hand and arm were healing slowly and with continued care it would be healed and functional again. Beth's ankle still carried several tones of color, but the swelling was going down and she was hobbling around in the barn with less discomfort. Sunshine loved having easy access to Beth's lap. She sought a chance to cuddle anytime Beth would permit. it

CHAPTER FIFTEEN   TIME TO HEAL, REBUILD AND RETHINK

Two weeks passed before the weather allowed Ben to start clearing the rubble out of the hut. The snow was melting and further delay would just make the job that much harder. He shoveled the dirt onto a hide and dragged it to the woods and dumped it in a neat pile. He searched through the dirt as he went so they wouldn't permanently lose anything. He started at the door and worked his way to the back. Progress was slow. He pulled a few pieces of very dirty clothing from under the mess.

His sister's doll lay buried under his old pants. It had somehow remained intact and fairly clean through it all. Once again he picked it up and tucked it into his shirt.

When he did, tears came unbidden to his eyes. That doll represented Sarah and finding it again, opened the door to the longing and need to find her. His emotions were raw and would be concerning her, until he could be with her again. He scrubbed his eyes with his sleeve and was glad that no one was there to see him. He worked furiously for a few minutes, taking his frustration and emotional pain out on the dirt that had tumbled to the floor of his hut. As soon as we have this hut rebuilt, I am going to take Ginger and look for her, he promised himself.

He had thoughtfully asked Jed to put the horses out and to make a big pot of buffalo stew that he loved. That way he was helping without misusing his injured hand.

Beth had been busy humming and stitching ever since he had brought the material in the barn. She wouldn't show them what she was working on.

Ben hadn't forgotten the hood he wanted to make. The weasel fur was ready and hidden in the back corner of the loft. He had two rabbit furs with it. I'll turn the fur side on the rabbit skins and then make a wide strip around the front of the hood with the weasel fur. I think I should turn the bottom under and run a string through it, so she can pull it up snug, for when it is windy. He smiled to himself when he thought of the beautifully carved antlers, high in the pine tree. The snow had helped to further hide them.

By midafternoon, he had cleared the floor around the boulder all the way from the front door. I know it must be sitting on some of our things but I can't think what they are. I guess we won't know until we miss them. At least it landed between the two caches. His thoughts ran a conversation in his head as he worked to make order inside the walls.

At last he was at the point where he had to figure out how to remove the front wall and move it forward. I guess I should start by taking the door off, then the frame and work out from there. He found that it wasn't as difficult as he thought it would be. By the time Jed was putting the horses back in their clean stalls for the night; Ben had dismantled the front wall and lined the pieces up twelve feet in front of where it had been.

The stew was delicious. Ben had worked hard and was hungry. Jed was pleased that he had contributed in some small way.

Stump and Bold One came over to the fire to see if they were going to get a share of the stew they had smelled for hours cooking. Jed ladled some of the stew into Stump's pan and some into a waterproof basket that was nearby. He blew on them until he could hold his finger in it and it was just warm.

"We can't have you guys burning yourselves," he said as he set them down. He watched as they ate. "I never in my wildest dreams ever imagined that I would cook supper for a wolf." Rascal was trying hard to nose his mother out of the basket. Ben handed him a piece of jerky and lifted him onto his lap. He liked Rascal, for the same reason he liked Buddy. They both were very intelligent and high spirited.

When everyone had eaten and was sipping their coffee, Ben went to the door and pulled in a small basket of wild cherries that he had taken from the cache, before he left the hut.

"Surprise, I brought desert. They are sour. I tried one, but they are good to nibble on. I want to save some of the seeds to plant next spring."

Beth picked up a small amount of hay and began to weave a basket. She handled the dry grass carefully. It was harsh enough to cut if not handled correctly. Soon she had a rough, but serviceable little container.

"All cherry pits go in here," she announced. "Everyone think pie!" And they laughed and talked together easily as the night came softly and the lantern was turned down to a golden glow.

The snow had a new coating in the morning. It was just enough to make the world look beautiful again. The places that were starting to show mud were hidden. Jed said that he wanted to go hunting. Ben really wanted to work on the hut wall, but didn't want to be a disappointment.

"You don't need to come with me, Ben. I know you want to get back to working on the hut. I don't plan on shooting anything. I just want to see if I can find out where the wild turkeys roost. This new snow should help to show their tracks. That way maybe we can get a fresh turkey for Thanksgiving this year."

"That's a great idea! And if you promise to move slowly, so I can keep up I would like to come with you," said Beth. "I feel like I have not been out of this barn for years!"

"Are you sure you are up to it?" Jed asked tenderly.

"My ankle is much better and the snow will make the steps soft under my foot. I am going to get bundled up."

Outside, Beth raised her face to the sun, peeking through the clouds that hung low and gray in the sky. "Looks like it will snow again soon. We probably should keep an eye on the weather," said Beth.

"I didn't think we would need to go far. Let's just walk a little way up river and watch for tracks," said Jed. They didn't find any turkey tracks, but it was nice to be out walking together in the fresh cold air.

"Well if we don't do any better than this next time, we will have to have rabbit. We better head back," said Jed, putting his arm around Beth.

"It is getting colder," she agreed.

Ben was in the barn frying fish when they came in. "The old hole by the willow came through again. I caught five so fast I couldn't believe it. I was always told that fish are sluggish in the winter. They may have been lethargic but they were also hungry!"

"Ben, that smells delicious. Let's have some carrots with them." She went to the basket of carrots and pulled two big ones out, and stuffed the basket back in the hay. Washed and scraped, then sliced thin, they were put over the fire in a little water to simmer. Ben pulled the fish off the heat, so they wouldn't burn. "The carrots will take a little while. Tomorrow I want to bake some bread. I need to use the yeast so it doesn't die." "Beth where is the yeast?"

"I had it in a wooden bowl tucked in the side wall above the fire to keep it warm. I hope it isn't ruined."

"I hope it is still there! Ben, how is the wall coming?" Jed still felt strange not being able to work as a team.

"I have part of the wall extended near the triangle. I am still using wood that was in the roof. Soon I will have to start cutting some more."

"Maybe by then my hand will let me help. I hope so." Jed pulled on his coat and went to the hut. He brought back the bowl with the yeast ball in it. "It was right where you said it would be. It has dirt on the top but we can take that part off before you break it open to make the dough. I hope the cold hasn't ruined it."

"Thank you Jed for getting it. I have a big craving for fresh baked bread," said Beth. "I'm not sure how long it will take to rise or bake but I want to try tomorrow anyway. It can rest here near the fire until I need it. I am going to brush away the top and crack it open just enough to add a little flour, sugar and a tiny bit of warm water in case it is hungry."

Just as the sun was coming up, they woke to barking and growling, down by the river.

"What in the world is going on down there?" exclaimed Jed. "We better go see." Both men pulled on their boots and heavy coats and grabbed their rifles as they left the barn and headed for the river through the trees. Just before Jed stepped into the clearing, beside the river, Ben grabbed Jed's sleeve and pulled him back, into the bushes.

Up river on the opposite side, the bank was busy with riders. It appeared that they were getting ready to leave.

As they peered through the trees, a gray smoldering stain marked the spot where a fire had been. An arrow lit beside Stump sending him scurrying into the trees and changing his barking to a low growl. He remembered the pain of the last arrow that had found its mark in his leg.

"It is strange that none of us, not even Stump, heard them last night," said Jed. "It is frightening to think that they could have found us asleep and we would not have known they were around," said Jed.

"I agree. We have been careless. We need to rethink what we are doing and start using the top of the bluff to check the area regularly," said Ben.

"Did you notice that even their horses are painted? That is a war party!"

"They are heading down river toward the settlement!" said Ben. His harsh whisper reflected the panic and anger that he felt.

"I need to warn the people!" said Jed. "If I can get through, the canoe is a lot faster than they will be. The river is open in the middle here, but that doesn't guarantee that it is all the way to the falls. When Beth and I were there the people were talking about the army building a fort near there, on the Silver. I wish they would hurry up about it."

"Ben I have got to go right now! You will have to take care of things here and in the name of "Jesus" take good care of Beth and keep her safe. Mark the path to the top of the bluff so you can climb it quickly and safely and use it. You can see for miles from up there. If it comes to that, turn the animals loose and go to that little cave in the bluff that we found. Stay there. I will find you. If you are gone from here, I will know where to look."

As they talked he had hurried to the hut. He was stuffing jerky and bullets in a bag. He filled the extra water bag and tossed them in the canoe as it rested in the hay in Ginger's old area. Jed put his rifle in beside the small quantity of supplies.

"Ben I need to go talk to Beth, but as soon as you are sure they are gone; take my canoe down near the water for me. I will only be a minute." Jed hurried away toward the barn, with Stump and Bold One right behind him.

"Beth, I have got to take the canoe and go to the settlement, right now! It was a war party that caused the barking. They are all painted and on the move across the river. They are heading down river! I think I can get there first to warn them if I hurry. Ben is going to use the bluff as a look out, and if he thinks there is danger coming, he will take you to a cave we discovered on our journey."

Her face grew pale as she clung to him.

"Jed, what if they see you? They will kill you! You can't try this. It is too dangerous. You don't know if you can get through. The river may be frozen over in places," she sobbed as she spoke.

Jed held her close for just an instant and then instructed her to prepare a couple of light bundles with anything that she and Ben would need in an emergency. You and Ben can go to the little cave, if it becomes necessary. He knows exactly where it is. I can find you there. Ben will be there with you. He will take care of you and protect you. Everything will be all right. Don't cry Honey. I love you." He kissed her and hurried to the water's edge.

Her face was white, and her hands trembled as she immediately began to follow his instructions. A tear slid down her cheek unnoticed as she remembered the raid on the wagon train and the merciless killings that took place. She knew that if they were found, they would be killed. She pulled her rifle to her side and checked to be sure that it was fully loaded. She was afraid for the first time since she had come to live here with Jed and Ben.

Ben stuck his head in the barn door.

"He is on his way. I slipped his supplies in the pillowcase and put the white sheet over him and part of the canoe. It will help to blend with the snow. I will be back in a few minutes."

Ben retrieved the extra rifle from the bedroom, and all the shells. He wanted to take them with him if he felt it necessary to leave. He wouldn't leave behind a gun or bullets that could be used against his family or anyone else. Ben returned to the barn adding them to the things that Beth had gathered. He placed the firebox next to the fire where it would be ready to prepare. He stayed only long enough to give her a hug and told Beth he was going up on the bluff to look. He took a spear with him, to feel his way through the snow that could hide a dangerous spot.

Once at the top, he looked at the river. Jed had already paddled beyond the bend and was out of sight. He is traveling with the current. That will help him, thought Ben. Please help him to get there in time to warn the settlement, he prayed silently. Far in the distance, on the edge of the prairie, looking like colorful specks, he could see the riders heading down river at a steady pace. They were not wasting any time. Jed would be faster on the river, but when he had to portage around the falls and the rapids, he would lose valuable time. He thought it would be a close race, and Ben wasn't sure which would win.

"Father, Please slow the riders and help Jed to get to the people in time. Please keep him safe." Ben's heart was racing.

The barn felt warm when he returned from the cutting wind on the top of the bluff. Beth had made coffee and cooked a pan of oats.

They ate quietly. Neither of them had an appetite. Beth's thoughts were of a time when she had stayed alone in a freezing cold cave. She didn't want to do it again. She was frightened for Jed and afraid that they might lose him and the life they lived here on the river. She loved it here and wanted to raise her baby, living with Jed, in a house on the hill by the lake. What would she do if the Indians spotted Jed on the river and killed him? She knew that she had to be brave and ask God's protection.

"Psalm 1:3, NIV says, "That person is like a tree planted by streams of water, which yields its fruit in season, and whose leaf does not wither. Whatever they do prospers."

"Ben, we have to claim that promise. Jed loves the Lord and reads the Word and obeys it. He follows the teachings of God. I have to believe that God will honor Jed's faith, and His promises. He will blind their eyes to Jed's canoe on the river. He will carry him swiftly on his way, while He slows the course of the enemy. He will surround our friends with an army of angels of protection, all this we pray in Jesus' holy name. Amen"

"Amen," said Ben.

Jed had to portage around the falls, but put the canoe back in the water at the bottom. He rode through the rapids at a furious pace. With no load other than his own weight and his rifle in the canoe it rode high in the water and Jed was an expert at controlling it.

The war party was forced to stop to rest their horses. They ate their travel cakes and believed they would be victorious when they arrived at the vulnerable, unprotected settlement. One of them joked.

"It was thoughtful of them to make a bridge for us to cross the Silver." They laughed, thinking the people would be easily conquered.

Jed arrived at the settlement by early afternoon. His arms ached from the over exertion. His burned hand was bleeding. He had not taken a break, buying the settlers valuable time to prepare.

Jed shouted as he ran toward the buildings. Men came pouring out in his direction. He quickly warned them.

"Jed I can only say, thank God that you saw them coming and had the courage to leave your family, to come tell us." Tom worked, with the others as he talked. The new, one rider, footbridge across the forked channels of the Silver River was built in sections. They were designed so they could be quickly dismantled and pulled to the settlement side of the river.

"They must have scouted the settlement and saw the bridge. They plan on riding right into the settlement. Otherwise they would have come across downstream where the wagons cross. Hurry men!"

Windows were shuttered. Animals were taken inside. Fires were extinguished and covered with sand. The town's activity disappeared. It was silent. The place looked deserted.

A man on horseback was sent racing up the Silver to warn the family that had settled at the spot where the wagon trains crossed.

Jed rested just a few hours and ate with Tom and Gentle Fawn. She coated his burned hand with a salve and bandaged it with soft cloth, wrapping it over and over to create a pad of protection as he pulled against the river's strength, heading home. They hugged him. Gentle Fawn was silent, but tears streamed down her face.

"I pray that God is with you, Jed." Tom whispered, as he pushed the canoe into the dark water and Jed headed home, away from the silent settlement. He had done what he could. The cover of night and God's grace saw him safely past the riders.

The sounds of the Indian war party drifted over the partially frozen river as Jed slipped quickly past. Each stroke of his paddle matched the cadence of his repeated prayer.

"Please God, protect them. Please God protect them."

He was back at the hut by early afternoon. Ben and Beth were amazed at the speed of his journey. He had carried the canoe around the rapids and up passing the falls at a run. Pulling against the current and tired muscles had slowed him some but once back in the water he continued to stroke until he was pulling up on the bank near home. He had made the journey in record time, driven by adrenaline and concern for his family's safety.

Beth, the expected baby, and Ben were his whole life; he had to be there, back where he could defend them.

Ben had seen the canoe coming. After running to the barn to tell Beth that Jed was safe and coming around the bend in the river, he waited in the trees where he knew that Jed would pull up. After a strong hug, he told Jed to go and Ben carried the canoe and its contents back to Ginger's area.

Beth wept with relief, as she looked at her husband, and ran into his arms.

"Oh God, You kept him safe. Thank you, Thank you." She said through her tears.

Day by day, they established a new routine. They continued to work on the hut and cared for the animals, but the ritual of frequent trips to the top of the bluff had become top priority. Extra care was taken to keep their home camouflaged from the river. The new front wall was against the pine trees that Ben and Stump had planted. Fires were kept small and meat was cooked inside. Even the odor of food could give away their position.

A rider from the settlement came to thank Jed and to bring news. The Indians had not attacked, but had turned away when they could not cross the Silver where it merged with the Hickory. Everyone wondered when the Indian scout had observed the settlement and the bridge that gave easy access. The family at the wagon crossing, farther up the Silver, had hidden, cold and frightened, for days in the woods, and had returned to a burned cabin, but none of their family had been harmed. They were staying with Rose, in the settlement, while Tom and the men from his saw mill helped build a new one. They had given up the land at the crossing and had exchanged it for a piece much closer to the settlement. The men all wondered why the Indians had not come to the settlement after crossing the Silver to burn the lone cabin.

Jed went hunting and shot a turkey for thanksgiving. They had much they were thankful for.

Ben and Jed worked harder at training Ginger and Angel to become good mounts. Ben was putting small bundles on Buddy's back by the end of winter, preparing for the day that they, all three, would have a horse to ride.

CHAPTER SIXTEEN   CHRISTMAS IN THE HUT

Now they worried more about their shots being heard.

They finally had to declare two days to work on their Christmas gifts, because their team spirit didn't provide them with time alone to do it.

They moved back into the new and improved hut, just a week before Christmas. The roof was supported with four beams. Logs stretched across a center beam covered with branches and willow matting, and then thatched grass. The piled dirt was tossed on top whenever a thaw allowed some of it to be freed from the pile. In spring more would be added. Soon it would match the sod of the prairie again.

Ben brought in a small Christmas tree and stood it in the corner. Once again they used imagination and crafts to decorate it. Crab apples were strung and looped around the branches forming garlands. They intended to string the popcorn, but it smelled so delicious when it was popped that they ended up eating the first batch. The second batch made it onto the tree. Beth surprised them with delicious treats. They sang songs, told old stories, and laughed a lot, but in the back of their minds hung the ever-present threat that Indians might discover them today. They gave and received gifts, but the one that was the biggest amazement, was the antlers that they watched Ben climb high into the snow covered pine tree, to bring down for Jed. The detailed carving was so tiny and so realistic that they talked about them the rest of the day.

Both men received brown hand dyed cotton shirts that Beth had sewn.

"You are an astonishing woman. When did you find time to make these?" Jed asked. She smiled but didn't reply.

Beth stayed in, out of the cold most of the time and found a need to rest more and more. Jed and Ben worried and fussed over her. They all prayed for her and the coming baby, asking God to strengthen her. Jed took over the cooking completely, saying he was bored and had to do something to be busy.

The tiny baby boy came very early, on a day when his first cries were mixed with the sound of thunder and pounding cold rain. His bright red color, pointed chin and bald head gave him a strange little old man look. Jed's hands shook as he delivered his first son. Beth lay on the old sheet that had been scrubbed and dried in the sun. It had been called into service one last time. Jed rejoiced at the birth of a new member of his family, but during the premature labor and moments when Johnny was actually brought into the world, he was petrified that something would go wrong. It was too soon. The baby was no bigger than his hand. He had seen a baby born when he had been traveling on the river. He had actually helped to deliver it. That baby had been larger, and looked healthy. Johnny was frail. Somehow, they muddled through. The tiny boy was diapered, wrapped tenderly in white flannel and placed against Beth's heart. Jed wrapped both of them snugly in bed where they could rest and be warm. Beth moved Johnny to her breast often. Each time he seemed content after nursing. He seldom cried and when he did it sounded like the mewing of a kitten.

Each day that went by gave Johnny a better chance at surviving, and every day they prayed God's blessing on him and thanked God for the little boy. Uncle Ben produced a beautiful cradle for him when he was just three days old.

"Your daddy and I will decorate it together sometime soon," he said. With all the mud that followed the early spring rains, Jed and Ben found plenty of projects they could work on in the barn. Jed made a rocking chair but when he sat in it he discovered that the rockers had to be longer or Beth might tip backwards. He tried again and after fitting on the new pieces, the chair rocked smoothly.

"Oh, this is perfect! Johnny and I will enjoy this," Beth said. She loved it.

They finally had the time, and made a table and benches. She was delighted.

"This is wonderful," she said as she spread the pretty red and white-checkered oilcloth on the table and commented how cheerful it made the room look. "Jed, someday we will have to have a kitchen in our house with a table and benches just like these. You are both so clever."

They made two bent willow chairs to use near the fire. Jed built a bed but kept it a secret, as a surprise for the new house he was planning for the coming summer. They took the parts up into the loft and slid them under the hay.

Next, they worked three days in a row putting two more cradles together. Ben and Jed carved and oiled them in the evenings while sitting near the fire. They would take them to the trading post when the trail condition was better.

Some nights Beth would read from the Bible while the two men worked, carving. Other nights they just sat sipping coffee or tea and telling stories of their lives, while Beth cuddled and rocked Johnny. He was slowly gaining strength and seemed to like the sound of voices near him. At two weeks old he gave his first precious smile to Beth as she changed his tiny diaper.

"Life here is a journey every day, without leaving," said Ben. "We are blessed to have each other and look at the life's journey this little fellow will have," he said, as he bent and placed a light kiss on the top of the baby's head. "The whole world is opening up for him to enjoy. The railroad will travel across the prairie by the time he is grown and he could ride from here to the east coast and back. I pray that he will never have the struggle we have had. He will have, **"The Land's Heritage**," and we will tell him our stories so that he will know God's goodness and as he grows it will be a journey with the Lord. And someday soon, I pray that we can all be here together," said Ben. They knew that he was referring to finding Sarah. They said, "Amen"

AN INVITATION

If you do not know Jesus, as your Savior, but you would like Him to be, please pray the following prayer. Invite Him into your heart. Commit your "New Life" to Him. He will be your constant companion, counselor, comforter, and protector. The Holy Bible tells us that He will never leave you or forsake you.

"Dear Jesus, please forgive my sins. Give me grace Lord, so that I will not commit them again. Come into my heart and strengthen me, so that I can start a "New Life" with you as my companion. I want to live according to your will and commandments. Bless me Lord and lead me in a life that is pleasing to you. In Jesus' Holy name I pray. Amen"

If you prayed that prayer, you are saved. You are born again. Your soul is whiter than snow. The angels in heaven are rejoicing as they write your name in the Lamb's Book of Life.

Get a Holy Bible and begin to read it. Sign and date the inside page as a witness for your new found faith. Tell someone! Find a good Bible believing church and start attending, so that you can learn more about Your Heavenly Father. What a wonderful God we have.

I will pray for you. God bless you. Louise Bouck

About the author

Louise Bouck is a follower of Jesus Christ. She has been married to her husband, Dale, for more than fifty years. Together they have raised six children.

Until an early retirement from her full time job at the Arizona Republic Newspaper in 2000, very little time was available to allocate for writing or art.

One of the many interests that Louise enjoys is painting on location. The lush greenery of Michigan, her home state and the abundant flowers in her grandmother's greenhouses and flower shop all encouraged her eye to appreciate the colors and beauty of nature.

Later after moving to Arizona, the rugged landscape of the mountains and desert stole her heart and took her artistic soul in a new direction. The move west inspired the location for her series.

Paintings in many media cover the walls of her studio as she has deliberately turned her creative side more to the written word. Hesitantly she withdrew from the art gallery where her work was sold and left the position of resident artist at the local Historical Society Museum.

Louise has written ten books in a series of Christian Bible based stories that she is now starting to release for the first time as she works on still another story and another painting.

Some of her work may be included as cover art on her books or as color plates of details from her paintings. She hopes that you will enjoy them all and be blessed.

Book titles in "The New Life Series"

- More than Survival

- Life's Many Journeys

- The Land's Heritage

- The Story of Sarah

- Together

- The Blue Stone People

- Teewahpanee the Boy, Two Feathers the Man

- The People of the Lion

- The Lion's Den

- Just the Beginning